Flint Book 7: The Finale

The Book That...

Flint Book 7:

The Finale

Treasure Hernandez

www.urbanbooks.net

Urban Books, LLC
78 East Industry Court
Deer Park, NY 11729

Flint Book 7: The Finale ©copyright 2010 Urban Books, LLC

ISBN 13: 978-1-60162-271-6
ISBN 10: 1-60162-271-6

First Printing June 2010
Printed in the United States of America

10 9 8 7 6 5 4 3 2 1

This is a work of fiction. Any references or similarities to actual events, real people, living, or dead, or to real locales are intended to give the novel a sense of reality. Any similarity in other names, characters, places, and incidents is entirely coincidental.

Distributed by Kensington Publishing Corp.
Submit Wholesale Orders to:
Kensington Publishing Corp.
C/O Penguin Group (USA) Inc.
Attention: Order Processing
405 Murray Hill Parkway
East Rutherford, NJ 07073-2316
Phone: 1-800-526-0275
Fax: 1-800-227-9604

Prologue

Two Months Earlier

Halleigh sat behind the counter, tending to her job at the Baltimore bookstore quietly, going unnoticed as she read a new novel. She had changed her appearance, so nobody who had ever known her before would be able to recognize her now at first glance. Her hair was cut in a short Nia Long style and dyed jet-black; her now studious look was a far cry from the glamorous wifey persona she had before leaving Flint. Her Gucci frames also helped to make her a new woman.

After escaping the misery that haunted them in their hometown, she and Malek were trying to piece their lives back together. Paranoia and the fear of being found plagued her every day. She was finding it difficult to adjust to her new life, and she wanted nothing more than to remain low-key.

It was a Sunday and Security Square Mall was unusually slow. She hadn't served a single customer all day, but she welcomed the peaceful environment of the black bookstore. She had no coworkers or nosy females around her trying to figure her out, so she was left to her thoughts.

She was trying to adjust to the East Coast lifestyle. The people there were much different than those from Flint, and Halleigh stood out with her Midwest twang and cold demeanor. Her hometown of Flint bred society's grimiest. Even the women had "an edge of callous" about them that was hard to shake. She was constantly on guard, which sometimes made people suspicious of her, and she had to remind herself that it was okay to be friendly to people she met in Baltimore.

It's okay to relax here. Nobody is going to find us. We picked Baltimore out of the blue, so nobody even knows where to begin looking, she thought as she stood to check the inventory in the back of the store.

As she did her weekly count, a chill swept up her spine, and the hair on the back of her neck stood up. She ignored the anxiety creeping into her soul because she knew nothing was wrong. She had to stop torturing herself.

She was so used to looking over her shoulder; she always felt like someone was out to get her. In fact, for the past few years there was always someone out to do her harm—Mitch, Toy, Manolo, Sweets, the feds. Every time she thought she was safe, someone came into her world and shattered her peace. Always. So she was always expecting the worst.

Just as she was about to shake the feeling off, she heard the sensor of the store ring loudly, indicating that someone had walked in. She put down the books in her hand and made her way back out to the front of the store. When she didn't see anyone, she froze.

Her brow furrowed as she stepped from behind the counter. "Is anybody here?" She began to look down each aisle of bookshelves. Oddly she received no response, but when she peered down the last aisle, she saw a girl standing there.

Halleigh froze instantly, paralyzed by fear, as she assessed the chick from behind. She remembered the description of Toy that Malek had given her, and this fresh chick with rock star–tight jeans, a cardigan, and long, silky braids seemed too familiar. Halleigh had never seen Toy personally, so Malek made sure to give her an accurate idea of what she looked like. She wanted to take off running, but instead she took a deep breath and spoke again. "Can I help you with something?"

The girl turned around and stared Halleigh directly in the eyes. Her gaze was intimidating, and Halleigh began to backpedal, her eyes darting for the door.

"What's wrong? Looks like you've seen a ghost," the girl replied as she approached.

Halleigh's eyes grew as large as saucers when the girl reached into her back pocket. She wanted to scream, but before she could open her mouth, the girl pulled out a book.

"I'm looking for the sequel to this joint right here." She handed it to Halleigh.

Halleigh felt like a fool for overreacting. *God!* She thought to herself. *Every gay girl with braids ain't Toy. Calm the fuck down.* She felt so foolish, her entire face turned red. She exhaled loudly and put her hand over her racing heart.

"Yo, ma, you a'ight?" the girl asked.

Halleigh nodded as she wiped away the tears that had accumulated in her eyes. "Yeah, I-I'm fine," she responded. "I thought you were somebody else."

"Somebody you not trying to see, obviously," the girl remarked with a smirk.

Halleigh didn't respond, ignoring the sarcasm in the girl's tone, and then proceeded to ring her up. Once she left the store, Halleigh collapsed into her seat. "You've got to get a grip, girl. Get a grip."

Finally closing time came around, and Halleigh couldn't leave the mall quick enough. Gripping her Mace in the palm of her hand and checking her back as she walked, she hurriedly located her car. Once she was safely inside she clicked the locks and drove to the apartment she shared with Malek.

As soon as she stepped inside the door, she saw Malek lying on the couch asleep. The sight of him was the only thing that made her feel protected. They had been through the storm for one another, and she loved him more than anyone in the world.

She dropped her bag onto the floor and walked over to where her man was sleeping. She crawled directly on top of him, and without thinking twice, he wrapped his arms around her.

"Shh, I just put li'l man to sleep," he mumbled. He gave her a quick peck on the forehead and went back to sleep.

Halleigh smiled as she thought about how lucky she was to have Malek and their son. She nodded her head and remained silent as she laid her head on his chest. For the first time all day, she felt safe as she drifted off to sleep.

A plague of guilt ate at Tasha as she leaned her head back in satisfaction as Toy took her to ecstasy. Their love affair consisted of nothing but sex, and being Tasha's first lesbian experience, Toy had easily blown her mind.

There was nothing that Tasha wouldn't do for Toy, so when Toy asked her to help find Halleigh, she easily obliged.

Tasha closed her eyes as Toy plucked at her love button, and enjoyed what she considered to be a little piece of heaven. Never in her life had any man stroked her this way. The treasure between her legs was like a ripe piece of fruit, and Toy was plucking it just right, her juicy lips sparking a flame in Tasha that she never knew existed, making her weak to Toy's deception.

Although Tasha was an exceptionally attractive young woman, Toy had many playthings. She had no desire for love. She was into head games, making her chicks do whatever it was she wanted and needed for them to do. Toy got high off power and control. The more, the better. The hold she had over Tasha was good for Toy's ego and very soon would satisfy her quest for revenge.

Toy had taken the death of her beloved brother Mitch personally. She hated to admit it, but beneath the hard exterior was a vulnerable sibling in deep mourning. On top of being disrespected my Malek, she felt robbed of the only family she had left, and because of that, Malek had to pay. She would go to all ends to ensure that he and everyone that he loved felt her pain, including Little Miss Halleigh.

Tasha had told her their entire history from beginning to end, at least all that she knew, and Toy knew that Malek and Halleigh were like a modern-day Romeo and Juliet. If she found Halleigh, she would find Malek. If Malek couldn't be touched, then certainly Halleigh could, and the blow would prove just as deadly to a man as deeply in love as he was.

Toy knew that their love would be their downfall, and she was waiting patiently to pinpoint their exact location. Halleigh had called Tasha once already, and Toy learned that the couple was hiding out in Maryland somewhere, but she needed a more accurate location before she could make her move. She wouldn't make the mistake of being overzealous and give them a chance to get away.

It had been six months since Halleigh's last call, but Toy waited. In the meantime she kept Tasha's head in the right place, making her wifey, sexing her right, and giving her a position to play, all of these things helping to keep Tasha in line.

Toy had done her research on Tasha before she had even approached her. She found out that she was one of the original Manolo Mamis, but her personality was strong, and she was no pushover.

Toy was an expert at the art of seduction. She knew what many men wished they did. She'd learned early on that every woman wanted to be a part of something. They all wanted to be down, and if you gave them that sense of belonging, they would be loyal. She had talked Tasha into submission, and now she had her loyalty. So when that phone call from Halleigh finally did come, Tasha knew what she had to do.

So as Toy went to work on Tasha, fulfilling her every fantasy, she was sure that sometime in the near future all of her efforts would pay off, and she would have Halleigh and Malek exactly where she wanted them.

As Halleigh sat with her baby son, Malek Jr., in her arms, she watched his father get dressed.

"You're going out?" Halleigh glanced at the clock, noticing that it was eleven P.M. She raised one eyebrow at Malek as she awaited his response.

"Yeah, I've got to hit the block," Malek stated, not noticing Halleigh's attitude.

Halleigh shook her head in disappointment. She hated the mentality that Jamaica Joe had instilled into Malek. The streets had ruined their lives in the first place. It had destroyed their plans of the good life long ago, and after escaping Flint, she thought that Malek would finally let them go. But she was sadly mistaken because Malek had dived full force into the Baltimore drug trade, blaming it on their situation, saying that he was doing it to provide for them.

True, their finances had dwindled, and they were barely making it when Malek decided to get back into the game, but Halleigh didn't care. The risk wasn't worth the reward. She had seen firsthand what that life could get you, and they had barely survived the first time. She wasn't sure they could deal with the ups and downs of the game again, but it was like Malek lived to hustle. It was in him like DNA. He acted as if he had never had a life before the streets began to raise him, and Halleigh felt like no matter how hard she tried to hold on, eventually she was going to lose him.

"I thought we came here to start over, Malek. I don't want you out there. This isn't our city. We don't know shit about B-more. We're supposed to be lying low," she reminded him.

"Don't worry yourself, Hal. I know what I'm doing. That li'l bookstore job you got ain't gon' pay the bills or put food in my son's stomach at night. I don't love what I do, but it's all that I got, so just trust me. I got you. I got us." He bent down and kissed his son on his head, then Halleigh.

Halleigh nodded and smiled a smile of uncertainty. She heard the words, but in her heart of hearts she knew Malek was moving all wrong. "I've just been feeling crazy lately. I'm constantly feeling like I have to watch my back. I have a bad feeling like something bad is going to happen or like someone is going to recognize us."

Malek shook his head and sighed. He knew the pressure of being on the run was getting to Halleigh. The stress was evident on her face. "You're just paranoid, ma. Relax. Nobody can hurt you from here. We're good. You're just thinking about the past too much. Let that shit go, Hal. Flint is miles away. And I know you don't like me hustling either. I hear you. Once I get my paper up, I'll stop. I promise."

Halleigh nodded. She walked Malek to the door and watched him until his car disappeared around the block.

She looked down at her son and cradled him gently in her arms. "Looks like it's just you and me today, baby boy," she whispered as she closed and locked the door.

As she looked around their small apartment, she couldn't help but think how their lives had come full circle. She had lived and seen it all. From the glamour and hood fame the game had to offer to the seedy side of life, she knew it in and out. Unlike Malek, she didn't miss it. She had a child to think about, and there was no way she was going to allow her child's life to be thrown off kilter the way hers was.

Halleigh sighed as she put her son into his crib for the night. Life in Baltimore was lonely, especially with Malek being constantly away from home. She had no friends, partly because she chose to keep to herself, but mostly because she didn't trust anyone.

But on nights like these when she had a lot of stuff on her mind, she needed someone to talk to. Someone she could relate to. Someone who had been through the same things as she, and would listen without judgment. *I miss Tasha,* she thought.

Although their friendship had been tested and stretched to its limit, it was the only one she had left. All of the other Manolo Mamis had been lost to the game, and at the end of the day, she and Tasha were the last two standing. In an attempt to separate herself from her old life, she had cut off all communication with Tasha, but as she sat in the empty apartment, the loneliness that crept into her soul made her yearn for her friend's understanding. *Maybe I'll give her a call,* Halleigh thought.

Chapter One

Tasha was feeding her nose the magnificent powder that Toy had introduced her to. She bent over the mirror and inhaled the lines of cocaine. She had never been addicted to anything in her life, but her new infatuation with white lines was slowly starting to grow on her. As she lifted her head, she pinched her nose and then snorted loudly, to stop her nose from running.

The ringing of her telephone interrupted her routine.

"Damn it," she mumbled as she stood to retrieve her cell phone out of her purse. Without even looking at the caller ID, she answered. "Hello?"

"Hey, Tasha."

When Tasha heard Halleigh's voice, she instinctively lowered hers. Toy wasn't even around, but she knew how long she had waited for that exact phone call. "Hey, um, hey. I know this ain't who I think it is," she responded.

"Yeah, long time no bullshit, huh?" Halleigh felt a sense of relief just from speaking with her longtime friend.

"What's up, Hal? I miss you, girl. You dropped that load yet?"

Tasha was making small talk in an attempt to keep

her on the phone. It was just her luck that Toy would be M.I.A. on the day Halleigh finally decided to call. The average girl would have felt guilty about setting Halleigh up, but Tasha was tired of being captain save-a-ho. Halleigh wasn't a naïve little girl anymore. She was grown as hell, and it was no longer Tasha's responsibility to guard her.

Tasha had done it in the past because she felt responsible for Halleigh's downfall, but it was a new day, and the way Halleigh had easily forgotten her brother, Tasha's loyalties lay with no one but herself.

"Yeah, we have a six-month-old son," Halleigh answered. "I was just thinking about you. I know we haven't talked in a while, and at first I was trying to cut all my ties to Flint, but you're all I got, Tash. You're my girl, and even though I know I have Malek, sometimes I just need my girl, you know."

Tasha could hear the sincerity in her words. She shook her head. *This bitch. That's why her ass always getting caught the fuck up. She's too fucking soft.* Tasha put her hand over her mouth and yawned, bored with Halleigh's overemotional rant. "Yeah, I hear you, hon. Well, you the one who went into hiding. I feel you needing to leave the city because of your situation, but dang, girl, you didn't have to shut me out."

"I know. Everything just happened so fast."

"Well, where are you? We need to get together. I definitely want to see your son."

Tasha could hear her indecision through the phone. She waited anxiously. She didn't want to seem too anxious about getting Halleigh's location, to avoid arousing her suspicion. She cleared her throat. "You know what, Hal . . . it's cool, babes. I understand why you don't want nobody to know where you are. I just thought we were better than that."

"Tasha, it's not like that. If you can get to Baltimore, then I'd love to meet up with you."

"Baltimore, huh?"

"Yeah. You got a pen?" Halleigh asked, not knowing she was about to give her enemy a one up on her.

Just as Tasha got up to scramble for a piece of paper and a pen, Toy walked into her home. She put her finger up to her mouth to signal her silence.

"Hold on, Hal," Tasha said, looking Toy in the eye. Toy smiled devilishly when she heard the name.

After finally locating a pen, Tasha said, "Okay, girl, where do you want me to meet you? Just say when, and I'll be there. I got a new man that'll give me the money to get there."

Halleigh arranged to meet Tasha that weekend at The Cheesecake Factory in downtown Baltimore. It was a public place, and she figured it was the safest way for them to reunite.

"Don't tell anyone you're coming to see me, Tash. Not a single person. Just get ghost," Halleigh stated seriously.

"I got you, Hal. I'll be there. See you Saturday," Tasha replied before hanging up the phone.

Tasha turned to face Toy and held the piece of paper up in her hand. "Who did that, mama?" she asked seductively, feeling proud that she was able to give Toy what she'd been fiending for.

Toy grabbed the paper out of her hand and looked at the rendezvous address. "You did that, ma." She planted a deep kiss on her lips, pushing her toward the bedroom.

Tasha had earned the orgasm that Toy was about to deliver. Now Toy could concentrate on the day she would face the bitch-ass nigga that killed her brother and finally bring him his fate.

Chapter Two

Scar Johnson and Derek Fuller sat across from each other in a small Italian restaurant just outside of Baltimore in a small town called Bowie. They always met there to avoid being seen together, which would be bad for their business arrangement. Baltimore was their stomping ground, so when they met, it had to be discreet.

Scar Johnson was a well-known kingpin throughout the inner city of Baltimore. He got the nickname Scar because of the long mark that went across his face. With his deep voice and built stature, the streets feared him, and the women loved him. All the makings of a street legend.

Fuller slid the rare steak into his mouth while listening close. He had a neat goatee and a lean build. He wore a leather coat and neat slacks, and looked like a cop. Maybe that was because he was one. Fuller was the head of the Baltimore Narcotics Unit and also partner in crime with Scar. Their operation was flawless. He was assigned to take down Scar, but in actuality, he was helping him, making Scar untouchable.

Scar said to Fuller, "Yo, I'm hearing a lot of noise about this new kid named Malek. He is fucking with my money. He's a out-of-town nigga trying to move in on my territory. He is selling coke at a cheaper price and taking away all of my clientele. My young boys are saying that our fiends are leaving our block to go fuck with him."

"So this li'l nigga is a problem, huh?"

"You damn right," Scar shot back. He had seen his money drastically slow up, and it became a problem that needed to be solved quickly. "Shake things up a little bit. Get the rundown on the nigga."

"I got you," Fuller answered confidently. "I'm on it today."

After discussing other matters, they exited the restaurant and headed back to Baltimore in separate cars.

Malek held Malek Jr. in the air as he looked into his son's eyes, seeing his own features. He glanced over at Halleigh as she sat at the vanity mirror combing through her hair, getting prepared for work. Halleigh didn't have to work by any means, but Malek let her because it kept her occupied and busy.

"You sure you don't want me to take Junior to the babysitter?" Halleigh applied some lipstick.

"Naw, I'm good, baby. I'm not going anywhere until you get back. He's cool here with me. Aren't you, li'l man?" Malek munched on his son's fat jaws.

Halleigh smiled and admired the way Malek was so close with his son. She knew he was a good man and would always protect them. She was with the man of her dreams and wouldn't trade it for anything.

But as you know, trouble always seemed to find Halleigh and Malek, so just because they had moved to Baltimore, shit didn't change. Just the scenery.

Chapter Three

Halleigh sat in the busy Inner Harbor restaurant waiting patiently for Tasha to arrive. Her son sat in his car seat, which was atop the table. Anxiety filled her stomach as her foot tapped nervously on the floor. She was knocking at the devil's door by reopening the line of communication with Tasha. She knew the risks, but at the same time needed a friend, so she felt that it was a risk worth taking.

Like always, Malek was in the streets, but on this day she welcomed his absence. She didn't want to tell him Tasha was coming to town. He would flip if he knew Halleigh was meeting with her, so she kept this to herself.

Toy eased her car into the downtown traffic as she and Tasha approached the restaurant. "Don't be too pushy with her. Act like you are really here for a reunion between old friends. I don't need to make my move today. I just want to watch her and see if she leads me back to that bitch-ass Malek. When the time is right, I'll make my move."

"How long should I tell her I'm in town for?" Tasha asked as she pulled out a small baggie of powder cocaine.

"Slow down on that shit. I need you on point for this."

"I'm always on point." Tasha continued her get-high routine, vacuuming the coke up her nostrils. "Just drop me off at the corner. I'll call you before dinner is over, so you can be ready to pick me up."

Under normal circumstances Toy would have just snatched Halleigh and tortured her until she gave up Malek's location, but the young girl was a bit brighter than she had anticipated. As Toy looked at the crowded tourist area, she realized that Halleigh had chosen a place where nothing could go wrong. Too many witnesses.

Tasha emerged from the car and headed into the restaurant. Not a flicker of remorse crossed her mind as she stepped inside. It wasn't hard for her to spot Halleigh. Although her appearance had changed and she had put on a couple pounds of baby weight, Tasha could spot her a mile away. Her body language and gracefulness hadn't changed.

Halleigh breathed a sigh of relief when Tasha finally walked through the door. The bad feeling that had been lurking in her heart immediately disappeared when she saw Tasha wave and smile. She stood to greet her with outstretched arms.

"Hal!" she screamed, not caring about the other patrons in the building.

"Hey, Tasha," Halleigh replied as they held one another and rocked back and forth affectionately. "It's good to see you, girl."

Tasha immediately focused her attention on Halleigh's son and her heart could not help but skip a beat at the innocent face. "Oh my goodness. He's beautiful, Halleigh."

"Thank you." Halleigh pulled him from his seat and handed him off to Tasha.

Tasha held Malek Jr. in her arms as she took a seat. The amount of love she felt from the baby boy surprised even her. She had to hurry up and get him out of her grasp before her conscience started eating at her. She was, after all, plotting on his mother and father. She handed Halleigh her son, and Halleigh put him back in his seat.

Halleigh discreetly zipped his diaper bag to conceal the .45 handgun she had taken from Malek's closet. She had brought it with her for protection, just in case, but now that she was face to face with Tasha, she didn't feel the need for it anymore.

She sat down, and after a round of drinks, they were chatting as if no time had passed them by. It seemed so genuine to Halleigh, and for the first time in months she felt normal. There was no need to peek over her shoulder every few minutes, no anxiety, no paranoia. She was relaxed and social. Finally she was able to let her guard down.

After sitting for hours, she checked her watch and noticed how quickly the time had passed.

"I've got to go, Tash. But how long are you in town for?"

"A few days."

"Well, we should get together again before you leave. I work at this mall out here called Security Square Mall. I'm working tomorrow, but you can stop by if you want. I know you're always in the mood to do some shopping." Halleigh laughed.

"Definitely. I'll call you."

The two girls hugged once more before Halleigh wrapped her baby securely and left.

A bored Detective Maria Rodriguez sat back in her unmarked car and watched the restaurant. She hated to get stuck with the uneventful stakeouts. While the rest of her squad was busy tailing their mark, Malek Johnson, she had drawn the short stick and was instructed to follow his girlfriend. The only female cop on the task force of the Baltimore Narcotics Unit, she was used to being put on dummy missions and knew at first glance that Halleigh was a dead end. The girlfriends never lead you to anything. As she sipped her coffee, she knew this stakeout was a waste of time. She picked up her squad car radio so she could two-way her partner.

"Hey, numb nuts. I hope you know you owe me dinner for this one. There's nothing going on my way."

"Just stay on the girl. There's a big reward in it for everybody if we stop this young boy in his tracks. Just play your position, Rodriguez," Detective Derek Fuller replied, reminding her who was in charge. "Everybody has a position."

She sucked her teeth and gave him a few choice words

in Spanish before refocusing on the task at hand. Just as she was tempted to pick up the newspaper from her passenger's seat, she finally saw movement from the entrance of the building where the restaurant was located.

She watched as Tasha exited the restaurant first. The detective silently admired the glamorous clothing and jewelry. *These young girls walk around here with no job or education. All they have to do is snag a hustler or baller and they live the lavish life.* Here she was working a nine-to-five and could never afford the high-end designers that graced Tasha's body. That was the reason why she never felt bad about the drug dealers that she and the rest of her Narcotics Unit colleagues chose to extort. That leveled the playing field. And, unfortunately for Malek, he had come to town and stepped on the wrong toes.

She observed Halleigh as she retrieved her car from the valet. The detective started her own vehicle to prepare to set up her tail, but she fell back when she noticed a black Charger pull out behind Halleigh. She followed three car lengths behind, to stay undetected. She ran the plates and discovered that the car was a rental.

"Looks like somebody else is interested in this girl too. Maybe there is more to her than meets the eyes," the detective mumbled to herself.

She flowed with the traffic, making sure she made every light, to keep up with the two cars ahead of her. Something was up. She wasn't sure exactly what it was, but she didn't want to overplay her hand before she figured out what was going on. *This girl doesn't have people following her for nothing. What type of shit is she into?* Detective Rodriguez's instincts told her that Malek and Halleigh were into something other than the petty drug game.

"What the hell? Is this the same Charger that has been behind me since I left the harbor?" Halleigh tried to peer through the windows of the car, but the limousine tint didn't give any indication of who was inside. Her heart began to beat as her foot got heavier on the gas pedal. "Maybe I'm just being paranoid," she tried to convince herself.

To test her suspicions, she got off the highway and rode through the city streets, redundantly hitting for lefts. She hoped that the car behind her wouldn't follow suit, but her fears were confirmed when she made her first turn.

Detective Rodriguez fell back as she noticed Halleigh begin to drive in circles. *She knows she is being followed.* "She's not as dumb as she looks," the detective commented to herself.

She patiently waited at the corner to see how the situation would play out. Her stakeout had ended for the day, but she would start again first thing in the morning because now she wanted to know who else was on Halleigh's trail, and why?

***

After realizing she was being followed, Halleigh jumped back on the expressway and headed in the opposite direction of her home. No way was she going to lead someone back to the place where she rested her head. She sped up, pressing her car to the max, hoping to shake whoever was on her ass.

"Fall back, Toy! She knows you're following her."

Toy, her eagerness for revenge making her foot heavy on the gas, ignored Tasha.

"You think she's going to lead you to Malek now that she knows we're behind her? Halleigh's not dumb. She's not going to put that boy in harm's way. She'll die herself before she lets anything happen to him! Fall back. I'm supposed to call her tomorrow. We can catch up with her then."

Toy reluctantly slowed her car down. She was too close to let her temper blow her plans now.

Chapter Four

Scar and Fuller were set again to meet at the small restaurant in Bowie. On the way to the spot, as Fuller drove up, he began to feel guilt for playing on both sides of the law by being a cop and partner with a drug dealer. But Scar and Fuller had a relationship that went much deeper than what appeared on the surface. They were blood brothers. Derek Fuller thought back to how thier partnership came about.

"Mom!" Derek screamed, his small, angelic face turning flush red as he jumped up and down in sheer terror. His brother stood next to him and peed on himself as he watched too.

"I told you before, bitch. You don't play with my fuckin' money!!" a strange man screamed as he dragged their mother by her hair.

The man was so big, and his skin was so black; to Derek he looked like a giant monster.

As the boys screamed, the man hoisted their mother in the air by her throat.

Derek felt vomit creep up his throat, and his bowels threatened to release from the fear he felt.

His mother clawed at the man's hands in a futile attempt to loosen his grip so she could breathe.

"Get off my mommy!" Stephon screamed, the scar he was born with dragging the side of his mouth down, causing his words to slur.

Derek grabbed onto his little brother's shirt and pulled him back. He couldn't risk this monster harming his brother too.

"Please don't hurt my babies," their mother rasped, begging the man for mercy.

"Bitch, you should have thought about that before you decided to cross me," the giant said, hoisting her up and throwing her up against the wall.

She hit the wall with a thud and slid down, her body going limp like a rag doll. She continued to scream and beg for her life as the man pounded on her, his fist landing at will, each punch harder than the one before.

"You like to smoke crack? You like to steal from people, bitch?" the man growled as he lifted her weak body up so he could get to her face. With the force of a Mack truck he backhanded her, sending one of her teeth flying from her mouth. Blood covered her face and hugged the floor around her. "Now, I expect to get my money by tomorrow, or you and these bastard trick babies of yours gonna be dead." The man spewed a wad of spit on her crumpled form.

Five-year-old Derek and his four-year-old brother Stephon cowered in a corner, with Derek trying to shield his brother from harm, as usual. Although he was only five, Derek often acted as if he were ten or eleven. On the nights his mother disappeared or stayed holed up in her bedroom with different men, he would pour cereal or make a sandwich out of whatever was there for him and his little brother, who his mother had nicknamed Scar because of his misshapen head and the scar that dragged down one side of his face, making his head resemble a boulder. He would make sure his brother washed his face and brushed his teeth before they went to bed.

"Rock-a-bye baby, on the tree top," she would sing to her younger son. She would call Derek her "baby genius" and tell him he was destined for greatness.

People often thought Derek and Scar were fraternal twins because they were the same size. Although Scar was a year younger, he was always just as big as Derek.

When he was sure the giant was gone, Derek got up and went to his mother's side. "Mommy?" He nudged her frantically. He thought she was dead for sure. "Mommy!" he called out again, urgency rippling through his words.

Finally his mother shifted and winced in pain. Then she moaned and turned over. Struggling to get up and barely able to speak through her swollen lips, she rushed her boys to put on their coats.

Afraid and visibly shaken, Derek followed his mother's instructions and helped Scar into his coat and put on his own. Their battered mother rushed them out of the apartment, looking around nervously the entire time. Once they were outside, she let her motherly instincts take over. She ignored the massive pains ripping through her entire body and walked at a fast pace to get her children far away from the potential danger.

Derek could keep up, but Scar had a hard time, and he gasped for breath because he had to jog just to keep in step.

After walking for what seemed like an eternity, the trio finally came to a middle-class white neighborhood that Derek had remembered passing on numerous occasions and wishing he lived there.

"Go in there, and y'all stand right by that green dumpster. Don't move until I come back. You hear me, Derek?" his mother said, her words garbled and her face becoming more swollen by the minute.

"When you coming back?" Derek asked, shivering.

"Take care of your brother, okay? He is special, and don't you let nobody bother him about his face. You hear me?" Her body quaked with sobs.

"When you coming back?" Derek asked her again, an ominous feeling taking over him.

His mother shoved them along. "Just take care of your brother."

As they started ambling forward slowly toward the dumpster, their mother turned and limped away, her heart breaking as she went farther and farther away from them. She knew somebody would find them there and take care of them. She feared that if she had kept them, her addiction would've eventually gotten them killed.

Scar began crying out, "Mommy! Mommy! Don't leave us."

"Shhhh! Mommy is coming back. I'm gonna take care of you until she comes back," Derek consoled, squeezing his brother's hand tight.

Derek took his brother and stood right where his mother had instructed him. They stood at the dumpster until the sun came up, and their legs throbbed. Scar whined and cried the whole time, between nodding from sleep deprivation. Derek refused to sit down or allow Scar to sit down. His mother had told him to stand there, and he would not let her down. Several people passed them and stared, but no one said anything to them. It was the trash truck driver who came to empty the dumpster that finally asked Derek why they were there.

"My mommy said she is coming back for us," Derek had said.

After waiting with Derek and Scar for three hours, the trash man finally called the authorities, and Derek never saw his mother again.

When Child Protective Services workers and the police showed up, Derek still refused to move. "No! I'm waiting for my mommy! No!" He screamed and kicked to no avail.

They had to physically remove him from the dumpster, and he and Scar were whisked away to the hospital for a medical clearance and then off to foster care, where they remained for over a year.

With the mandatory expiration on parental rights, after eighteen months, they were put up for adoption. Every Wednesday, Derek and Scar went to the agency along with about twenty-five other kids for display for prospective parents. Derek would always hold Scar's hand and secretly tell people that they were not going to be separated, and that if they wanted him, they would have to take Scar too.

With one look at Scar's disfigured face, the potential parents always turned away and found other kids to adopt. Derek's plan had worked for weeks, and each week he and Scar would go back to their foster home.

After a few weeks, the social workers couldn't figure out why at least one of the boys couldn't attract an adoptive family. The workers finally started sitting close to Derek and Scar and listening to what Derek was saying to the people shopping for children. When the workers got wind of what he was doing, the following Wednesday they put him and Scar in separate rooms, and Derek was picked immediately. He was seven, with the cutest dimples and the prettiest smile. Scar, on the other hand, had been overlooked again and again.

The day Derek's new family came to pick him up—a father who was a cop and a mother who was a teacher—he refused to leave without his brother. He had fought and cursed and even locked himself inside the bathroom.

The social worker had lied to Derek to coax him out of the bathroom so his new parents could grab him and get him home. "Your brother will be coming along soon," she said. "Go ahead. You'll see him again."

Derek reluctantly went. He wouldn't see his brother for another fifteen years, by which time they had both landed on opposite sides of the law.

In Derek's new adoptive home, everything seemed to be perfect. His father fought crime, and his mother taught him everything there was to know in any book imaginable. They were a real family. They ate dinner together and had fun movie nights on Fridays, his father's day off.

Derek lived like a kid that had been born with a silver spoon in his mouth. He wore the finest clothes, had every toy before it even became popular with other kids, and most of all, he had a real family life with both parents.

But everything wasn't as peachy as it seemed. Derek's father worked the midnight shift, and when he left home at ten o'clock after tucking his son in and kissing his wife, things would take a dark turn in the house.

Derek's adoptive mother would creep into his bedroom at night and shake him awake, standing over him in a see-through nightgown. Longing for her husband's touch and affection, Ms. Fuller was lonely and desperate. She would climb into bed with her adopted son and stroke his hair. Then she would tell Derek that she loved him more than anything in the world, and that if he wanted to see his brother again, he would have to touch her and she would help him find his brother.

At first it started out as touching. She'd take his little hands and guide them around her body. She would make him touch her breasts and put his fingers in her vagina. And by the time Derek was eleven, she had begun to make him have full-blown intercourse with her. She would always perform fellatio on him first then make him perform cunnilingus on her. Then she would take his still growing penis and force him to put it in her sloppy, oversized pussy. Most of the time Derek felt disgusting and dirty; sometimes he wanted to vomit.

But as the years went by, things changed and he felt differently. His body would betray him, and he started to experience sensations he didn't quite understand. Derek had conditioned himself to fight the good feeling that he started to get as he got older. He told himself the faster he got to that feeling the better, because his turmoil would be over. Derek would ejaculate after a few minutes, so he wouldn't feel so guilty. It was ingrained in him as a coping mechanism. "Come quickly, and it will be over," he used to tell himself.

Although at his adoptive home in the posh northern Maryland suburb of Bowie; Derek had every toy, private school education, went to church, and lived in a beautiful home, none of it was good enough. All he wanted was to see his biological mother and brother again.

Meanwhile, Scar remained in the foster care system in the hood of Baltimore. After years of enduring teasing and beatings at the hands of other kids in group home after group home, Scar grew angry inside. On most days he felt ruthless and often had visions of killing the social workers and the other kids with his bare hands. It wasn't long before Scar was on edge.

"Hey, ugly," a boy had called out to Scar one day, throwing a ping pong ball from the day room and hitting him in the head.

Scar bit down into his cheek and ignored his tormentor.

"You so ugly, we could probably win a world war just by showing your face to the enemies." The boy continued garnering laughs from the other kids sitting around. "Look at that scar and those saggy lips. I bet your mother must have fucked a gorilla to get something as ugly as you." The boy let out a shrill, grating laugh.

That was it. Scar snapped. His ear seemed clogged, and the room started spinning around him. He'd never tolerated anyone talking about his mother or his brother.

"Arrrggh!" Scar screamed out, suddenly lunging at the boy with a pocketknife he had stolen. Scar had buried the pocketknife deep into the boy's neck, hitting his jugular vein.

The boy's eyes popped open in shock. He didn't expect the "ugly monster kid" to ever fight back. Screams erupted in the room, and some of the other kids ran out into the hallway to get help, as the boy backed up from Scar's contact, holding his throat and gagging.

Scar stumbled backward at the sight of the boy's thick burgundy blood spewing like a fountain from his neck. Before any of the group home administrators could help, the boy bled to death within minutes, right at Scar's feet. And though Scar was scared to death, something inside of him felt powerful, almost invincible. The group home security quickly tackled Scar to the floor and held him there until the police arrived.

Scar spent two months in a mental institution because of that incident. After the psychiatrist cleared him, he was placed in a juvenile detention center, where he stayed until he was eighteen years old. It was at the detention center that Scar learned all of his criminal ways, so by the time he was released onto the streets of Baltimore, instead of being rehabilitated, he had become a ruthless dude with a nothing-to-lose attitude.

***

Derek went away to college and only returned to his adoptive home when his father was laid to rest after a long battle with cancer. When the funeral was over, he told his adoptive mother she would never see him again.

He had never forgiven her for years of sexual abuse, which had followed him like a looming nightmare. He always felt like he had no control over his own body or his own sexuality. When he began having sex for pleasure with girls his age, his body would betray him. His body would overpower his will not to ejaculate quickly.

Derek immediately moved back to Baltimore. Maybe, just maybe, he would run into his real mother or his brother.

After a year of looking for corporate jobs, he joined the Maryland State Police, hoping to become a state trooper. He had long since given up the active search to find his mother and brother again. In fact, he didn't know the first place to look. Checking the foster care system had turned up nothing on Scar. Those records were sealed on kids that aged out of foster care anyway.

Then one day, as a highway patrol trooper, he walked into the squad room of the Narcotics Unit to get a white powder test done on a substance he had seized during a car stop, and right on the wall was a huge poster with his brother's face and name plastered on it—WANTED: STEPHON "SCAR" JOHNSON, REWARD $10,000 He stared at the picture for what had to be ten minutes. When it had finally sunk in that the man in the picture was really Scar, Derek got so nauseated and weak, he almost threw up.

"What's the matter, Fuller?" one of his colleagues asked. "You look like you saw a ghost in that mufucka, Scar Johnson."

"Nah, nah. Just looking around," Derek said, quickly pulling himself together before anyone caught on to his interest in Scar. After seeing that picture, Derek was hopeful again, and he set out to find his brother.

When he pulled Scar's criminal history, he learned just what his brother had been doing since he had last seen him at five years old. Scar had a rap sheet as long as a city block. Derek learned that Scar had become the founder of the notorious Dirty Money Crew, a crew of killers that had murdered their way to the top of the Maryland drug trade. Though Scar was on the other side of the law, being his blood, Derek was still determined to find him one day.

Derek worked hard to prove himself as the best trooper on the streets, just so he could get enough clout in the department to put in his application to join the drug team. He was a man on a mission. After six months, he made the Narcotics Unit, officially becoming a jump-out boy. Every time he went out on a jump-out operation to pick up the hand-to-hand street pharmacists, he was hopeful he would run into Scar or get some information on him.

Finally, Derek and his team jumped out on a set of corner boys, and it just so happened the little dudes they picked up were down with the Dirty Money Crew, and low men on Scar's payroll. It didn't take long for Derek to get one of them alone and promise him freedom if he told him where to find Scar.

At first, the little soldier was living by the street creed—

No Snitching! But the longer the boy sat in a cell, unable to use the bathroom, get anything to eat, and with no phone calls, he finally gave in and provided Derek with the information he needed.

Derek had sat undetected outside of all of Scar's trap houses for weeks, but Scar never showed up. Being out there, he figured out every drop-off and pick-up time. He had numbered Scar's workers and tried to figure out who was a higher-up, which meant he was probably closest to Scar. Derek noticed one particular dude as the most consistent player at all of the trap houses, and he never stuck around long. Derek reasoned he was the lieutenant, in charge of bringing the re-up and picking up the profits.

Derek decided to tail him, and sure enough, one night he followed the dude right to his leader. His heart thumped wildly when he peeked out of his windshield and saw Scar in the flesh. There he was, his long-lost brother, all grown up and the leader of a crime syndicate. Derek could recognize that scarred face and huge head anywhere.

Both proud and sad, he wondered what their lives would have been like, had their mother not abandoned them that fateful night. He figured the big-ass man that had beaten his mother unmercifully had probably returned and killed her, and he had long convinced himself that she was probably better off dead than running the streets chasing crack.

Derek had watched Scar that first night without revealing himself, although he wanted to rush out of the car and embrace his brother with a big hug and a sincere apology. He didn't know how his brother would react to him, or if he would even remember him. Conflicted, Derek went home to his then girlfriend, Tiphani, and confided in her: He was a cop and his brother was a wanted criminal. Tiphani told him to do whatever would make him happy.

For two days Derek changed his car and disguise and watched his brother. Finally, he felt he had grown the balls to reveal himself to Scar. He walked up to Scar's bar and lounge, Katrina's (named after their mother), which also housed Scar's office in a secret room in the back. He was stopped at the door and asked what his business was, since it was a bit early for patrons.

"I just wanna get a drink, man," Derek said to the goons protecting the front door. Long fuckin' day."

The front door man surveyed Derek, trying to see if he could tell if this square was a cop or fed. Since he was dressed like a typical street dude, Derek was allowed entry.

Derek ordered a few drinks to build up his courage. "He's your little brother," he whispered to himself, "li'l Scar head."

Walking to the back of the lounge, Derek encountered yet another layer of security, a tall, muscular dude.

"Yo, man, I need to see Scar," Derek said to the dude, trying to sound as street as he could. Derek had lost that edge a long time ago, so it was a stretch for him.

"Who the fuck are you, nigga?" the goon asked.

"Tell Scar I got information on his family."

The goon crinkled his face in confusion. Everybody on the street knew Scar always proclaimed he was a pure-bred street nigga born from the concrete. No mother, no father, no family.

"Nah, Scar ain't got no family," the goon told Derek.

"Everybody got family. Now tell him I got information on his family," Derek said forcefully.

Scar's security guard reluctantly went behind the secret door, which was obscured with police grade double-sided glass. Two minutes later, the man returned and said to Derek, "Scar wants to know, if you got information on his family, where was his mother's birthmark?"

Derek swallowed hard as his mother's face came flooding back to his mind's eye. He could see her brown sugar–colored skin and straight white teeth so clearly smiling at him, but those memories were from a time when things were so good for them. The last time he'd laid eyes on his mother, though, she was a gaunt skeleton with missing teeth and riddled with bruises.

Shaking his head left to right, Derek tried to get it together. "It–it was a heart-shaped, cherry-colored mark on her left cheek," he said, barely able to get the words out, "and she used to call it 'a mother's love' and tell us she got it from our kisses."

The man was really confused when Derek said "our kisses." He looked at Derek wildly and then disappeared. Within minutes the man returned, and Derek was allowed to follow him back to the secret office.

When Derek stepped into the room, it was like time stood still. Scar was sitting behind a huge mahogany desk like the CEO of a legitimate company, his face looking much improved. His scar actually made him look dangerous, instead of ugly and deformed like it did when he was a kid. Who would've thought an ugly birth defect could benefit him? Derek, thinking his eyes were deceiving him, was at a loss for words as he stared at Scar, and his legs grew weak, threatening to fail him.

"Ain't this a bitch! My big brother," Scar said, standing up and stepping from behind the desk.

Derek was still speechless. He didn't know whether to cry, scream, or say sorry.

"I know the cat ain't got your tongue, nigga. You ain't happy to see your little brother after a hundred years and shit?" Scar grabbed Derek for a manly hug.

"I'm just so fuckin' happy to see you, man," Derek, shaking all over, finally managed to say. "I'm so sorry I couldn't keep my promise at the time. I was a kid. They snatched me away from you. I had promised Mommy—"

"C'mon, man, I don't hold you responsible for nothin'. Them white people ain't care nothing about two black little niggas tryin'a keep whatever piece of family they had together. I ain't never blame you, my nig. Besides, if shit didn't happen the way it did, I wouldn't be the king I am today." Scar offered his dumbfounded brother a seat.

"I told Mommy I would always take care of you. I'm back and I will keep that promise," Derek assured his brother.

And he wasn't lying. Although he had pledged to uphold the law of the State of Maryland, Derek had another chance to keep his promise to his mother and he vowed he would forever be his brother's keeper—if his brother wanted to be kept. From that day forward he helped Scar stay one step ahead of the law. One step ahead of the jump-out boys and the narcs.

But when the heat got turned up on Derek to make some big busts, he spoke with Scar, and they agreed to put on their little show. Scar agreed to take a fall to help his brother look good in the eyes of the department and the public. That's why Derek Fuller would always be grateful to his brother and never forget the sacrifice he'd made for him.

Chapter Five

Halleigh sighed in relief when she saw the car diminishing in her rearview mirror. Her heart was still pounding in her chest. She peered in the backseat to check on her son and saw that he was sleeping in his car seat. He had no idea what had just gone down, and frankly, neither did Halleigh. She knew this was more than her being paranoid. Somebody had tried to follow her home. She didn't know who it was, but she was sure she was in danger. She could feel it in her bones that something bad was lingering closely and she had to let Malek know.

"Malek!" she yelled as she raced into the house. "Malek!" She went through their apartment, turning on every single light in her home. Her distressed yelling caused her baby to begin to cry, and his wails filled the house. Realizing that Malek was nowhere to be found, she tried him on his cell phone.

"What's up, Hal?" he asked, upon answering.

"Malek, somebody tried to follow me home today!" she yelled, still in a panic.

"Halleigh, ma, we've been over this. Nobody is going to touch you here. Nobody's after you."

"Malek, I saw the car. I spun the block like you taught me. I'm sure—"

"Hal, baby girl, we'll talk about it when I make it home. You're safe. I'ma keep you safe, a'ight. I'm not going to let anyone hurt you again."

Frustrated, Halleigh hung up the phone. She wasn't as weak as Malek thought she was. Halleigh was hoping she could convince him to see things her way before things got bad and it was too late.

She securely locked the front door and checked every window before she staked out on the couch with her son lying on her chest, and waited for her man to make it home.

The next day Halleigh didn't even mention what had happened because she knew no matter what she said, Malek would simply brush her comments under the rug. She could feel him watching her with worry in his eyes.

"I'm fine, Malek," she said.

He stood and walked over to her, shirtless and sexy. "You've got to stop thinking that everyone is out to get you, ma. This is a new start for us, Hal. Nobody's gon' find us, and ain't nobody gon' touch you or my seed. I'll die first. I know Mitch fucked up your head when he took you, but I handled that. The nigga's a memory, but I can't fight your ghosts for you, ma."

Halleigh nodded as she rose out of their bed. "I've got to go to the bookstore today, baby. I'm working until close."

Halleigh left the baby with Malek and then dressed quickly before exiting the house.

***

Detective Rodriguez watched Halleigh emerge from her house. Today she was eager to follow the young woman. Whatever was going to go down with Halleigh, the detective didn't plan on missing it.

She followed Halleigh to Security Square Mall. She knew she was in store for a long day of waiting.

Work couldn't go by quickly enough for Halleigh, and as the mall closed down, she prepared to leave. The parking lot was dark when she stepped outside, and as she sped up her pace to hurry to her car, she didn't notice she had company.

Toy and Tasha sat watching Halleigh, but they in turn didn't realize that Detective Rodriguez sat at the south end of the parking lot watching them too.

Halleigh clutched her shoulder bag tightly, feeling the security of the .45 tucked inside. Her stiletto heels clicked against the pavement as she hightailed it to her car.

Feeling uneasy, she decided to make sure no one was following her before she headed home, so she pulled out of the parking lot and took the long way to her house, stopping to run a few errands on the way, all the while keeping her eyes on the same black car with Toy and Tasha.

"Fuck is this bitch doing? I'm getting real tired of playing cat and mouse," Toy stated.

Halleigh had pulled her card and was tired of playing games as well. She was done running and being the

victim. It was time for her to find out who was behind
the black tint. Her loaded courage was in her purse, and
she figured that whatever they wanted, it was going to
be handled tonight because she refused to bring the devil
to her front door. She had a son to think about; it wasn't
just about her. And whatever beef was looming in the
air, she was about to cook it.

Her pounding heartbeat drowned out the sound of everything around her as she pulled into the deserted lot
of a closed convenience store. Just as she predicted, the
black car was not too far behind. Tired of being prey to
this unknown shark, she got out of the car, clutching the
gun from inside her purse.

The black car parked at the other end of the lot in an
attempt to be discreet, but Halleigh had already peeped
game. There was no use in pretending. She wanted to
know who was inside the car.

She began to walk across the parking lot, and when
she was halfway to the car, she yelled, "Why the fuck are
you following me?" She attempted to put some bass in
her tone, but the quivering of her voice revealed her fear.

As she stood her ground, she watched as the car before her turned off its headlights, and a car door opened.

"Get out of the car," Toy said.

"What?"

"She trusts you. Get her to come over to the car."

Tasha watched as Halleigh held her ground in the
middle of the deserted lot. "And then what?"

"Then we make her take us to Malek."

Tasha had not planned on getting this involved. She had helped Toy find Halleigh and had even lured her out of her hiding place, but now Toy wanted her to basically help snatch her off the street. She started to say no, but the venomous look in Toy's eyes told her that it was do or die. She sighed as she climbed out of the car.

"Halleigh!" Tasha exclaimed as she walked over to her. "I've been following you for twenty minutes! Why is your phone going straight to voice mail? I've been trying to get you to pull over for miles."

"Tasha?" Halleigh yelled in confusion. She sighed a breath of relief. "What the fuck are you doing? Why are you following me?" She threw her arms up in frustration. "You scared the shit out of me!"

"I went to meet you at your job, but you were pulling out when I was pulling up. I tried to call you and let you know I was behind you, but your phone was going straight to voice mail." Tasha knew her excuse was flimsy, but she was hoping that Halleigh was still as naïve as she'd always been.

"Fuck, Tasha! You out here like a stalker. I didn't know who you were! Were you following me yesterday too?" Halleigh yelled angrily. She put her hand over her racing heart.

"What? Hal, of course not! Why are you spazzing on me? I just thought we could go out for drinks. You told me you worked at the mall, so I decided to meet you after work, but you got out of there like a bat out of hell. I couldn't keep up."

Halleigh nodded and calmed down a little, not wanting to overreact. She was the one who had invited Tasha to come to Baltimore to visit her. *She's your friend. Stop tripping.* She noticed the black Charger was still running. "Who's in the car?"

"That's my boyfriend. He flew in to surprise me last night. I want you to meet him." Tasha gushed. "Then maybe we can go for that drink?" She put her arm around Halleigh's shoulder. "It looks like you could use it, and someone to talk to. I know you, Hal. You're stressing about something."

Halleigh nodded and then stepped over to the car. It was comforting having her friend by her side. She began to doubt herself. *Maybe Malek's right. Maybe I am tripping.*

As soon as she stepped over to the car, Tasha pushed her from behind as the driver of the car stepped out and grabbed her neck violently. She looked into the eyes of the driver and knew she was in trouble. This was the girl she'd been running from. She didn't need an introduction. The menace behind her gaze told it all. Mitch's sister, Toy, was standing in front of her face, and she could see the rage, the hate, and the vengeance in her eyes.

"You bitch!" Halleigh yelled as she lunged for Tasha. "How could you! I have a son, Tasha! You dirty, grimy-ass bitch."

Toy slapped Halleigh across her face so hard, her neck snapped back, and stars appeared behind her eyes.

"Look, ma, I don't got time for this ra-ra shit. You know who I'm after. We could have avoided this entire li'l confrontation if you had just led me to the nigga, but you wanted to jump bad and play detective. Well, now you know who's behind the tinted windows, ma. Where's Malek?"

Toy spoke so smoothly, it almost sounded like she was trying to seduce Halleigh rather than threaten her. She did not need to raise her voice to get her point across.

Tasha said, "Halleigh, just tell her. You heard what she said. She ain't worried about you. She only wants Malek. That high-school love bullshit is played, and you know it. Stop being stupid, and think about what's best for you. Do yourself a favor and just tell her where he is."

"Fuck you! I'm not telling shit. You dyke-ass bitch, you'll never get to Malek."

There was no way she could tell Toy how to find Malek. That would be putting her son at risk, and he always came first.

Toy punched Halleigh in the face with so much strength, it sent her to the ground. She popped the trunk of the car. "Get the fucking duct tape out of the back of the car," she told Tasha.

Halleigh held her face as she rolled onto her side. "Aghh! Shit!" She spat blood out of her mouth. She opened her eyes, and the first thing she saw was her purse lying next to her. She remembered the gun was inside, and without thinking, she jumped at the opportunity. She reached inside the purse for the gun, wrapped her hands around the trigger, glad that she had left the safety off, and aimed at Toy's chest and fired.

Bang! Bang! Bang!

Chapter Six

"Oh, shit!" Detective Rodriguez shouted as she watched gunshots erupt through the parking lot. The yellow flicker from the burst of the gun lit up the night like tiny fireflies. She knew she should have intervened when she first saw the situation get out of hand.

When she saw Halleigh aim her gun again at the other girl, she didn't hesitate to turn on her lights and swoop down over the lot. She sped up directly to the scene and hopped out of her car, her weapon drawn.

She aimed her well-trained shot at Halleigh. "Baltimore Police!" she yelled. "Put your weapon down! Now!"

"You dirty bitch! I trusted you!" Halleigh shouted at Tasha, who stood with tears in her eyes, and her hands in the air.

"Hal, don't do this. I didn't have a choice. She was going to kill me, Halleigh," Tasha lied. "You have to believe me."

"Halleigh," Detective Rodriguez said calmly, "I need you to put down your weapon. One person has already been hurt. Let's make sure everyone else goes home tonight." The detective could feel the animosity in the air.

"You were supposed to be my friend," Halleigh cried, snot dripping from her nose. She was hysterical, and her hand was shaking. Everything inside of her wanted to dead Tasha where she stood. *She deserves it,* Halleigh thought as her finger played with the trigger.

"Hal, it's me. I'm your friend," Tasha said. "You know I wouldn't do this to you unless I had no choice. She was threatening me."

"Friend?" Halleigh shouted. "Bitch, you call yourself my friend? Yeah, Tasha, you're my friend, my ace boon coon, bitch! The same friend who helped Manolo manipulate me when I was just an innocent teenage girl. The same friend who sat by and watched me self-destruct on heroin and cocaine? Yeah, bitch, you're my friend, and if that's how we do, then you deserve every one of these bullets. They all have your name on them!"

It was obvious that Halleigh was letting out all of the resentment she'd held inside over the years.

"Halleigh, if you pull that trigger, then I have to pull mine. The first murder can be justified. It was self-defense; you were protecting yourself. I saw it. But if you kill this girl, there is no turning back. You will be a murderer, Halleigh."

Halleigh's resolve began to break, and she began to lower her arm, but just as she was about to drop the gun, she noticed the smile that came across Tasha's face. The smile enraged her. It was smug and arrogant, as if Tasha had never even expected her to be a threat. Halleigh lifted her arm and fired a shot into Tasha's face, erasing her smile forever. Then she immediately dropped the gun and put her hands in the air.

"Get on the ground! Now!" Rodriguez yelled as she kicked Halleigh's gun away. "Face on the concrete!"

She shuffled over to Toy's body and checked for a pulse. After feeling none, she felt for Tasha's. Both women were clearly deceased, and now she had to clean this situation up. She didn't want Halleigh in jail, and she definitely didn't give a shit about the two dead black girls lying beneath her feet. Her and her team wanted Malek. Now she had leverage to hold over Halleigh's head to get her to help them get him.

She put a crying Halleigh in handcuffs and then pulled her forcefully from the ground. "You have the right to remain silent. Anything you say or do can be used against you in a court of law. You have the right to an attorney. . . ." The detective read Halleigh her rights as she pushed her toward the unmarked squad car and secured her in the back.

"Damn it!" Rodriguez slammed Halleigh's door shut. "Damn it!" she yelled again, hitting the trunk of the squad car. Now she had to figure out how she would clean up this mess she had allowed to happen.

Malek wasn't even an official case. It was one of their underground hustles, actually a favor to another drug dealer. Malek was competition, so he had to go, but things were going farther than they ever had before. Every cop bent the rules, but this was clearly breaking them. Two bodies would not be easy to cover up.

She trotted back over to the murder scene and discreetly picked up the murder weapon. She wrapped Tasha's dead fingers around it and shot the weapon once. She then did the same routine with Toy to ensure there was gun residue on the girls' hands so that when the coroner bagged and tagged them, there would be no suspicion of a third party being present. She definitely wasn't going to be the one to call it in. Someone would happen upon the bodies in the morning. For now, she had a hustler's wife to crack.

As Halleigh sat in the back of the squad car, being escorted to the police precinct, she knew Malek would be looking for her. *What have I done? My baby,* she thought. She knew she was on her way to prison for a very long time. She had shot two people in front of a police officer. She felt that today was her judgment day, and didn't think there was any way she was getting out of this one.

When they arrived at the police station, Rodriguez escorted Halleigh inside the building. Choosing to bypass processing, she took her to a private room where there were no two-way windows or video cameras. Whatever was said, only the two of them would hear, which was exactly the way Rodriguez wanted it.

She pulled out a wooden chair and sat Halleigh down.

Halleigh winced when her bottom hit the seat. Her hands were twisted behind her back, and the handcuffs were uncomfortably tight on her small wrists. "Can you loosen these cuffs?"

Rodriguez obliged, knowing it wasn't going to take the bad cop role for her to get Halleigh to see things her way.

Halleigh gazed at the floor silently, thinking about her fate.

Detective Rodriguez let Halleigh's imagination run wild and left the room to give the tension time to build. The more nervous, the more on edge, the more afraid she was, the better. This was the best type of informant to have, one that had something to lose.

Half an hour later, Rodriguez came back into the room. By this time Halleigh's eyes were red and puffy from crying. The left side of her face was swollen, and she had a busted lip from where Toy had punched her. Her bouncing leg let Rodriguez know that she was ready to crack.

Rodriguez pulled out a chair and sat across from Halleigh. "You're in a lot of trouble."

Halleigh remained silent as she wiped her eyes with her hand. *I don't need this bitch telling me what I already know.* "I want a lawyer," she replied between sniffles.

"Even if Johnnie Cochran arose from the dead to represent you, he couldn't get you out of this one. You murdered two people, Halleigh, in front of a police detective."

"I didn't have a choice," Halleigh responded drearily.

"You have one now."

Halleigh looked up at the detective and shook her head. She knew the look in Rodriguez's eyes well. She wanted something from her. It was the same thirsty look that Manolo had given her, that Mimi used to possess.

"You being there tonight wasn't a coincidence, was it?" Halleigh asked as tears built in her eyes. She felt like this entire situation was a setup.

"I have been following you for the past few days, Halleigh."

Halleigh balled her fists and put them to her forehead. She knew she wasn't crazy. All this time her intuition was right. Running, hustling, surviving since she was seventeen years old, she was tired, exhausted at this point. Now here was one more person looking to use her in some way.

"What do you want?"

"I want your boyfriend Malek."

"Malek?" Halleigh whispered back almost breathlessly. It was like no one in the world wanted them to be together. There was always a situation threatening to tear them apart. *What the fuck is this? National fuck over Malek day?* "What do you want with Malek?"

"That isn't a concern of yours. All you need to say is yes or no. You can help me and my people gather our evidence against him. I want to know where his money is, what type of business he's into, and who he is doing it with."

Rodriguez stood up. She put her hands in her pocket, revealing the gun and badge hanging off her belt. She circled Halleigh as she continued. "If you cooperate with us, I can make this predicament that you've gotten yourself in . . . disappear."

"Disappear?" Halleigh repeated skeptically.

"*Poof!*" Rodriguez opened her hand as if she were performing a magic trick.

Halleigh's heart ached as she closed her eyes. She loved Malek. There was no way she could turn her back on him now. They were soul mates. They were meant to be together. Their destinies had always been intertwined, and she could never see herself turning on him. They had been through everything together. The good and the bad, they had experienced it all, and still found their way back to one another. There was always treachery around them, and now this woman wanted her to create deceit from within. Obviously Detective Rodriguez didn't know their story. She didn't know their Flint tale and was unaware of the type of love they shared.

"I can't," Halleigh said. "I would never—"

"Why? Because you love him?" Rodriguez laughed as she removed a picture from a large manila folder she was holding. "We've been following him too, Halleigh. You want to know how he spends his days?"

The detective placed a picture on the table in front of Halleigh. It showed Malek going into the home of a young dark-skinned girl's brownstone. "You want to know how long he stayed?"

"About three hours?" Halleigh rolled her eyes.

Halleigh wasn't studying that photo. There was nothing that this cop could tell her about her own man. She knew the little broad in the photo was the girl who cooked up Malek's work. Malek had personally introduced the two and had sought Halleigh's approval before he even started doing business with the chick. Malek was always honest with her, and between them lay no secrets. She leaned forward and slid the picture back across the table.

"I'm not talking, so do what you got to do to me," Halleigh stated, remaining strong on the outside, but on the inside she was crying out.

Detective Rodriguez had underestimated Halleigh's

loyalty to Malek, but she had a trump card in her deck. She was sure her love for her son was much deeper than the one she felt for Malek.

"Are you really prepared to go to jail for life just to protect your boyfriend? Halleigh, what about your kid? Because if I turn you in, Halleigh, I can guarantee you will never see the light of day again." Detective Rodriguez could see Halleigh's heart breaking as her mind raced. If the world wasn't so cold, she would've felt bad about what she was doing.

"I see a hundred girls like you every year, Halleigh. They stand by their drug-dealing boyfriends through it all. They give up their freedom, their children get sucked into the system, and for what? For nothing, Halleigh. Even if we don't get to him through you, we will get to him eventually. He's in love with the streets, and they all fall. And when he does, we will be there to catch him. So you might as well save yourself now. If you don't care enough about freedom, care enough about your child to make the right choice."

Detective Rodriguez was plucking at the heartstrings of a good mother. As much as Halleigh wanted to be strong, the tears falling down her graceful cheeks were giving her away. This wasn't how things were supposed to go down. Their love story was meant to end in a happily ever after, not like this. No matter what decision she made, her son Malek Jr. would be losing one of his parents. Either she was going to prison for murder, or she was sending Malek in her place.

"Why are you doing this to us? I don't know nothing

about some kingpin bullshit. There is no money, no cars, no nothing. We're not even from here. We're just trying to live."

"You should have stayed wherever you came from then, Halleigh. This is Baltimore, and let's just say Malek has stepped on the wrong toes," Rodriguez admitted, finally feeling bad for the love-struck girl.

Halleigh ended the conversation, refusing to speak to the detective any longer, but Rodriguez was patient and knew that time would crack Halleigh.

Hours passed before Halleigh realized she had been backed into a corner. She loved Malek and always would, but she couldn't see herself leaving her son. It was no longer just the two of them. She had their son to think about, and he needed her.

She stood and went to the locked door that held her confined inside the room. She kicked the door and yelled, "Rodriguez!"

Detective Rodriguez re-entered the room and waited for Halleigh to speak.

Halleigh put her hands on top of her head. She couldn't believe what she was about to do. "Aghh!" she screamed in agony as she closed her eyes tight. She wished that when she re-opened them she would be awakening from a bad dream. "I'll do it," she said, barely audible.

"Excuse me?"

"I said I'll do it!" Halleigh shouted.

It was three o'clock in the morning, and all Halleigh wanted was to go home. Malek had probably lost his mind with worry by now, because he had been expecting her hours ago.

"I need to call him."

Rodriguez leaned across the table. "You will tell him you were carjacked. We brought you here to file a police report. That's the story you will tell him. We will return your car to you tomorrow and say we found it abandoned somewhere."

She began to break down the specifics of what she expected Halleigh to do, how she wanted her to record conversations that would help them take Malek down.

Halleigh barely listened. It was late, and she was overwhelmed, while exhaustion wrecked her. On top of that, her stomach was hollow from the blood on her hands.

"I can't do this right now. I said I'll do it, but I need to get my head together. I just want to go home," Halleigh whispered.

Rodriguez was eager to get down to business and irritated that Halleigh wasn't listening.

"Please," Halleigh pleaded. "We can meet the day after tomorrow at my job."

"Fine. But don't forget what is at stake for you. I'll still be watching you, so don't make this hard and try to run." Rodriguez stood. "I'll take you to use a phone."

When Malek raced into the police station with their son in his arms, Halleigh burst into tears.

"Keep it together," Rodriguez mumbled as she watched Malek approach.

Halleigh, unable to maintain her composure, ran to him and fell into his arms.

Malek held her face in one hand and caressed her

cheek gently. "Did they touch you?" he asked, pain and anger apparent in his voice.

"No, no, they just hit me when I wouldn't get out of the car," Halleigh lied. "I'm so sorry."

"What are you sorry for, ma? This isn't your fault. The whip can be replaced; you can't. I love you, Halleigh. I would go crazy if anything ever happened to you."

Detective Rodriguez walked over to the couple. She had an inside-joke smirk on her face. "Halleigh, I will be in touch," she said. She handed her a card. "You can contact me anytime if you need me."

Halleigh nodded, feeling extremely uncomfortable. "Can we get out of here?" she asked Malek.

"Yeah, let's get you home," he said as he kissed the top of her head.

Halleigh grabbed her son out of his arms and cradled him closely as she allowed Malek to lead her out of the precinct. She could feel Rodriguez's eyes following her every move, burning a hole in the back of her head. She began to cry softly.

Malek tried to give her space, figuring she was just feeling vulnerable because of her experience. He was supportive and told her that things would be fine, but on the inside he was furious.

Chapter Seven

Derek Fuller and his crew stood in front of Malek's crack house, all of them wearing concealable bulletproof vests. They were about to ambush his spot and shut down his operation.

After Scar had given Fuller the rundown on Malek, they immediately began to plot. Scar wanted Malek's upcoming business to be stopped before it got too big, so Fuller grabbed his trusted squad and set up a raid to try to scare off Malek.

"One, two, three," Fuller said as he watched as his crew hold the battering ram, preparing to cave in the door.

On cue, they burst through the door and rushed into the spot, guns drawn.

"Everybody on the floor!" Fuller yelled as he rushed in.

What he saw blew his mind. The house was empty. Only a single card table sat in the middle of the floor. It had Fuller confused, and he and his crew stood there scratching their heads.

"Fuck!" Fuller turned around in a full circle, scoping out the room. "Bullshit!" He kicked over the table.

"Somebody must have tipped him off." He shook his head from side to side, his hands on his waist.

Malek sat in his crack house as he observed his youngsters cook, cut, and package the coke. He had set up shop in one of his many spots earlier that day. Malek never stayed in a spot for more than a week, and luckily for him he'd evaded the cops by the skin of his teeth without even knowing.

Malek saw the money going through the cash machine and got a flashback to when he was getting money in Flint. He took a seat at the table and got a bad feeling. He didn't get into Baltimore's drug game to take it over. Just enough to stack a little paper and then retire from the game for good.

He went into the back room where his right-hand man, Dayvid, was at. "I got to let this shit go," he said to him.

"We just got started," Dayvid said, loading the duffel bag with money as it came out of the machine. "You going to let all of this shit go?" He looked at him with a furrowed brow.

"Yeah, I got a shorty to think about. I never wanted to stay in this shit. I'm just trying to stack a little paper and bounce. I'ma hand this shit over to you."

"Word?" Dayvid said, liking the sound of what Malek had just said to him. Dayvid was only nineteen, but by being under the wing of Malek for the past year, he grew up quick. Malek had taught him everything he knew and was molding him to be a kingpin.

"You ready for this?" Malek asked.

"I was born ready."

"Oh yeah, I almost forgot." Malek dug into his pocket and pulled out a small box and tossed it to Dayvid.

Looking up, Dayvid reacted quickly and caught the box with one hand.

"Happy birthday, my nigga," Malek said, releasing a rare smile.

Dayvid smiled. He was totally taken by surprise that Malek even knew it was his birthday. Dayvid had no family and never received anything for his birthday, so he never saw it coming. He opened the box and exposed the diamond pinky ring and slowly nodded his head in approval as he smirked.

"You want to be a boss, right? Well, you have to start looking like one," Malek said as he stood up. "Let's roll," Malek said as he headed toward the door.

Later that night Scar was lounging in the VIP section of the club with his crew as they did every Friday night, bottles of liquor and strippers surrounding them as they enjoyed themselves. They were on the top level, which gave them a clear view of the main floor, and the loud bass from the club's speakers had the club rocking.

Scar stood at the glass front and looked down at the floor, watching the stripper on stage shake her ass.

His goon squinted his eyes and noticed Malek in the corner of the club with his crew. They were showering the strippers with dollars, and all eyes were on them.

"Yo, Scar, I think that's the nigga that's been moving weight on our turf. The one with the black fitted hat on."

"You sure that's him?" Scar looked down at the man in question.

"I'm positive. There is his li'l man, Dayvid. The one that's making it rain."

"Send him a bottle of Mo and then tell him I want to holla at him."

Scar was a good businessman. He knew that beef wasn't good when making money, so he took the peaceful route, and decided to make Malek an offer to get down with his squad.

"Cool," Scar's goon said as he grabbed up a couple of niggas and headed down to confront Malek.

Scar rubbed his hands together. *Young stupid niggas always trying to make a come-up*, he thought as he smiled to himself.

Scar had learned earlier from his police informant that they had just missed Malek when they raided his spot, so he decided to step to Malek and offer him a position on his team. He'd been in the game too long, and he knew how to muscle people with his money. He was going to make Malek work for him and make him think he was a business partner.

Malek sat back and watched as his li'l man enjoyed his birthday. Although Malek was in the midst of half-naked women and his niggas, he was only thinking of Halleigh and his son.

Just as he formed a slight smirk, he noticed three men approaching the booth that he and his crew were sitting in, and immediately Dayvid and company stood up and went for their guns.

"Whoa, whoa! Hold on, fam. We come in peace, fam," the goon said, holding up the bottles of Moët in his hands.

Dayvid put his hand on the chest of the head goon as they were headed straight for Malek. "What the fuck is the problem?"

"First, get your fucking hand off my chest," the goon said to Dayvid as he looked down at his hand. "Second, we're not coming over here on no beef shit," he added in a non-confrontational tone. We just wanted to talk to your boss, that's all."

"Let 'em through," Malek said, sitting back and watching the scene unfold.

Dayvid stepped to the side and let the goon through, leaving Scar's other two goons standing at bay.

"What can I do for you?" Malek said as the goon sat across the table from him.

"Scar sent you these bottles of Moët and wants to have a sit-down with you."

"Sit down with me?" Malek then paused. "For what? We don't have anything to talk about," he said calmly.

"That's for you and him to discuss. I'm just the messenger."

"No, I'm good right here. Tell your boss he can keep those bottles too. As you can see, we have our own bottles." Malek grabbed a bottle of Dom and took a swig.

Malek didn't even give the goon a second look as he focused on the stripper on the main stage, and the goon slid out of the booth and headed to Scar to tell him the news.

Malek had heard about Scar, but didn't feel the need to make any new friends. He sat back and continued to enjoy himself.

Not even ten minutes later, he saw the same group of men approaching his table again, but this time they had another person with them. It was Scar.

Malek's crew all stopped partying and slid their hands down to their waists as the crew approached. Scar's crew was notorious for busting their guns, so Malek's squad wasn't going to take any chances.

But Malek knew who Scar was, so he immediately told his crew to fall back and relax.

Scar came humbly and stood at the table with both of his hands collapsed into each other, in a non-threatening approach. "Hello," Scar said as he looked Malek directly in the eye with a small smirk. "I hear you're making a lot of noise in the streets."

"That's what you hear, huh?" Malek answered as he returned the stare. "I don't know what you're talking about, homeboy. I'm a working man."

"Please don't insult my intelligence, young brother. I'm not here to rain on your parade. I just want to give you a business proposal. I see you recruited my li'l man Dayvid, huh? I raised that nigga!"

Dayvid just stared at Scar with hateful eyes and never said a word. They'd had a past relationship that was a story of its own. Although heated by Scar's comment, he remained silent and played his position.

"I'm listening." Malek had already made up in his mind that he wasn't going to deal with Scar, but he would hear Scar out, so he wouldn't seem like he was blowing him off.

"I see you moving heavy coke. I know that I can beat your supplier's price. If you cop from me, I can keep the local police off your crew . . . and protection." Scar quickly grew a more sinister look on his face at the end of his statement.

"Protection?" Malek smiled as he sat up from his slightly slumped position. "Protection from who?" he asked, feeling the tension coming from Scar. "That sounded like a threat more than a proposition."

"You can take it how you want," Scar said, tired of playing games.

"Good day to you, sir," Malek said as he focused his attention on the stripper a couple of feet behind Scar.

Scar turned around to see what Malek was looking at. He chuckled, not believing Malek's arrogance. "You have a lot to learn, youngblood. Do you know who the fuck I am?" Scar asked, his jaws clenched tight.

Malek's crew acted accordingly to Scar's comment, and they all began to slide their hands to their waists, where their guns were, and Scar's crew followed suit.

Scar nodded his head slowly and stared at Malek intensely. He was growing more furious by the millisecond. He chuckled and then looked around at his crew, who all had ice grills and were ready to shoot on command.

"Let's go," Scar said, already having plans for Malek.

Scar turned around and left Malek and his crew alone. Scar's crew followed him. From the look on Scar's face, they knew what was to come next: *He don't want to get with the program, so he about to get shut down.*

"This is my city!" Scar mumbled as they made their way out of the door, cutting their night short.

Malek and his crew sat back and laughed at Scar's proposition and continued to have a good time.

An hour had passed, and it was approaching one A.M. Malek was taking shots with Dayvid, celebrating his birthday. Little did they know, Scar and his crew had no intentions of letting them leave that club alive on that night.

"This whole shit about to be yours, son," Malek said as he raised his glass and downed a shot.

"You're going to let all of this money we getting go?" Dayvid asked, not understanding how anyone could fathom an exit when business was booming.

"Yeah, I have been there, done that. I came to B-more to escape the street life, but it's so alluring, ya know. It seems as if the game just pulled me back in," Malek said, dropping knowledge on his young protégé.

"I'm going to buy this club and set up a legit life for me and my family," Malek said.

Just before Dayvid could respond, masked men ran into the club with automatic assault rifles and began to send shots at them. The sound of the bullets zipping out of the guns and shattering mirrors caused the whole club to go haywire.

Malek's crew quickly ducked for cover and returned fire, trying to defend themselves. Dayvid caught a bullet to the shoulder, but still managed to bust shots back while escorting Malek to the back exit.

Seconds later the rest of Malek's crew came bursting out of the back exit, and they jumped into the Suburban that they came in.

"What the fuck?!" Malek asked as he sat in the passenger's side, taken completely off guard by Scar's ambush.

"Get in!" Dayvid yelled, revving the engine as he waited for the other crew to jump into the truck. Once they were all in, he sped off, leaving tire marks on the back parking lot pavement. They had to leave and regroup. Scar had just started a war.

Scar sat back comfortably in an oversized Jacuzzi surrounded by three naked women, all sucking on different parts of his tattooed body.

The big plasma television that hung on the wall held his attention. He listened closely as the news reporter talked about the rising drug problem in inner city Baltimore.

Scar smiled, knowing he was the main cause of the drug problem in Baltimore, and by him having direct ties with the head of the Baltimore Narcotics Unit, he was untouchable.

He also knew shooting at Malek and his crew would lead to some sort of backlash, but he wrote Malek off as an amateur, which was a wrong move on his part.

Chapter Eight

The night was winding down, and Malek had just checked in on his sleeping son. Halleigh was lying in their bedroom, waiting for him. Malek had a lot on his mind, but didn't want to tell her about it.

He never wanted to bring his street business into his home, so he remained quiet about almost losing his life earlier that night. He instantly began thinking of ways to get back at Scar, but he was going to sleep on it, so he would make the best strategic move.

Malek walked in and looked at Halleigh and instantly wanted to make love to her. He sat on the bed, and she cuddled against him as he ran his fingers through her hair. He grabbed the remote and turned on the stereo. Classic Sade began to play.

Looking down at Halleigh as her head rested in his lap, all of his tensions melted away. Just being near her again felt good. He looked at her voluptuous figure and felt the swell of his dick rise against his jeans.

Halleigh sat up and straddled Malek, grinding her hips against his concealed manhood. She kissed him seductively, exploring his mouth with her tongue. Her body moved to the rhythm of the song, and Malek's hands gripped her breasts as they pressed against his chest.

Malek grabbed her backside firmly, and looked down at the thong that had disappeared in the crack of her ass. He pulled off the tiny thong and saw her fat lips soaked in her own juice.

Halleigh sat up. She couldn't wait for her man to please her. She reached for his belt buckle, and removed his jeans. His thick ten inches stood at attention in her face, and she couldn't help but to taste him. She devoured him into her mouth, making him disappear and re-appear over and over.

Malek placed his hands on her head and gently guided her as she sucked him like a lollipop. Halleigh's head game was superb, as if designed just for him. She ran her tongue up and down his length and kissed the tip gently, causing his toes to curl.

He pushed Halleigh back on the bed, and they got into the sixty-nine position. He opened her lips with his tongue and tasted her wetness as he licked at her clitoris, his tongue flicking back and forth, fast and then slow.

Halleigh rotated her groin, making love to Malek's firm tongue. The better he made her feel, the better she sucked his dick. She couldn't help it; he was making her go crazy and she wanted to suck him until he exploded.

Malek inserted two fingers into her pussy and shoved them into her like it was a hard dick. Moans couldn't help but to escape her lips as he tickled her insides with his fingers and massaged her clit with his tongue. She was riding his face like a cowboy, moving her head up and down like she was bobbing for apples.

Malek was large, and she wanted him inside of her, but she was feeling too good to stop him. He ate her out, and she hit him off until they both reached their climax. She swallowed his seed, leaving his dick spotless, arching her back as she came in his mouth. They both had reached ecstasy at the same time, releasing all of their pent-up tension.

Too exhausted to get up and do anything, Halleigh wrapped herself in Malek's arm.

"I'ma take care of you, Halleigh. You deserve the best, and that's what I'm gon' give you. That's my word."

"I already have the best. The world is ours, Malek."

Malek had to smile at her words. She was the perfect woman for him, and she would always hold him down.

"The world is ours, Halleigh. I love you, and after I get my dough up, we are going to relocate again. I am going to fly straight, I promise. No more hustling."

With those words they drifted into a comfortable sleep.

However, before he completely nodded off, Malek had figured out how he would strike back at Scar Johnson. He was going to hit him where it hurt the most. His pockets.

It seemed like the morning came too quickly because Halleigh was still groggy and exhausted from the night before. She felt the covers being lifted off of her and frowned as the draft of cold morning air caused goose bumps to form on her skin. She knew Malek wanted to pick up where they'd left off, but she was too tired.

"Baby, stop."

he has a lot to do with this. I asked you if
to get down; you told me no. I don't take
good, as you can see. Maybe you need
your answer. Right?" Scar gave Malek a
and then focused his eyes back on Halleigh's
y.

aybe I will reconsider," Malek said, telling
thought he wanted to hear.

car smiled from ear to ear as if they were
t's all I can ask for."

is crew headed for the door. He had no in-
lling Malek or his family on that day. He
send him a message. Wanted to let him
d be touched at any time.

were out of the room, Malek rushed over to
held her in his arms.

kay, baby?" he asked as he kissed her on
head.

med from Halleigh's eyes as she nodded
She then rushed into the baby's room and
alek Jr., who was sound asleep, resting
scooped him and kissed him, glad to see

Malek ran to the window in the living
Scar's black Navigator pull off.

lek screamed as he paced the room. He
put his family in the line of fire, and he
that. Scar had just made it personal by
me, breaking all the rules to the game.

to the back room, where Halleigh was
ing their baby close to her chest.

She felt him run his finger down her thigh.

"Malek, your hands are cold. Stop," she whined as she kept her eyes closed, not wanting to wake up fully.

It wasn't until Hal heard the shower running that she realized something wasn't right. The sound of running water sparked confusion in her mind. She sat up instantly to find three of Scar's goons standing in the room, one of whom was standing over her tracing the outline of her ass with a black .38.

"Ma—"

Halleigh tried to yell out to Malek, but before she could even get his name out of her mouth, a sweaty hand covered it, silencing her, and three pistols were aimed in her direction, the .38 pointed directly at her temple.

"Shut up, bitch," one of them calmly instructed.

Fear filled Halleigh's body, and her heart felt like it had sunk into her stomach. In any other situation she would have known how to react. She would have taken her chances and reached for the nightstand where she kept her .22. She would have warned Malek that someone was in the house. She would have done something.

But this situation was different. She had been caught off guard, and the goon that had the steel pressed to the side of her head intimidated her. There was something about the way that he looked at her that told her he wouldn't hesitate to pull the trigger. For the first time in a long time she was afraid.

She instantly began to think about her baby in the next room. She was hoping he didn't wake up crying and let it be known that he was there.

She didn't know what was going to happen or even why they had come. As the men's eyes ogled her body, she wanted to pull up the covers but was frozen in place.

Everyone in the room heard the running water stop.

The men cocked their weapons, and Halleigh's body stiffened when she heard the hammer to the .38 pull back. She did the only thing she could do and lifted her eyes to the sky and prayed silently.

Please, God, don't let them kill Malek. Please, don't let him come into this room.

Halleigh wasn't even worried about her well-being; the only thing she could think of was Malek. She didn't know what she would do if something happened to him.

Malek wrapped a towel around his waist and then made his way into the bedroom. He opened the door, and the sight of a gun threatening Halleigh's existence enraged him. He ran toward the bed but was halted by a bulky goon, who aimed a Ruger .357 Magnum in his direction.

"Malek!" Halleigh yelled out, afraid he would be shot. Her heart was beating like a drum, and tears began to swell in her eyes.

Malek's mind was focused on getting to her; he wasn't thinking about the hole that the Ruger would leave in his chest if fired. He grabbed the goon's wrist and punched him hard in the face, causing blood to flood from his nose.

"Aghhh! You muthafucka!," the goon yelled out in pain as he cupped his face with both hands and dropped to his knees in pain.

In one swift mover
from his hands and p
stood next to a terri
straight off of emotic
until he had his gun

Scar laughed as h
head. "Malek, what
perman now?" He c
stated, "Don't be st

Malek hesitated
were closed.

"What are you g
ing to kill me, Male
her brains will be

Malek dropped
had the gun on
making her dark
Malek even more
his jaw clenched

"Your girl has
Malek down.

Malek knew
leigh, so he kept

"You got out
want to kill yo
message."

"If you touch

"If I touch h
nigga?" Scar cl

"This has n
amongst ourse

"I think
you wanted
rejection to
to reconside
small smirk
exposed bod

"Yeah, m
Scar what he

"Great!"
friends. "Tha

Scar and h
tentions of k
just wanted t
know he coul

Once they
Halleigh and

"Are you
top of her for

Tears strea
her head yes.
checked on M
peacefully. Sh
he was okay.

Meanwhile
room and saw

"Fuck!" Ma
knew he'd just
couldn't accep
invading his h

He returned
crying and hol

"Baby, I'm scared," Halleigh cried.

Malek stood in the doorway, not knowing what to say to her to explain the ambush. "I know, I know," he said, trying to soothe her. He walked over to her and gently hugged her, with the baby between them. He softly kissed her on the forehead and let her know everything would be okay.

Malek was going to let the beef stay in the streets, but Scar had crossed that line. He relocated that evening, and quickly put a plan in motion. Scar was about to regret the day he stepped to him.

Malek set his goons loose on Scar's crew, orchestrating the robbery of six of Scar's main trap houses. He already had planned on doing it, but now Scar had just pushed up the date for it.

Malek's crew, led by Dayvid, managed to take close to $100,000 from Scar's various establishments. Dayvid knew all of Scar's spots because he, at one point, had planned on robbing them anyway. So when Malek told him about the plan, he was well prepared and informed about Scar's spots.

Scar's squad never saw it coming. This only made the beef between them more treacherous and heated. They now hated each other.

Chapter Nine

Halleigh's secret was too much for her to handle. As soon as they entered their home, she put their son in his crib and began to pace back and forth in their living room.

"Hal, you're home now. Come take a shower with me. It'll relax you. You need to get some sleep. You've had a long day," Malek stated.

So many thoughts were racing through Halleigh's head, she barely heard him. She was used to them solving their problems together, but on this, she was on her own. She had to find a way to come out of this without taking Malek down. Everything she had ever done was for him. She couldn't bring herself to deceive him, even though in her heart of hearts, she knew she had no choice. The decision had been made for her when she'd pulled that trigger.

Malek frowned as he approached her. He knew her like the back of his hand. There was something heavy on her mind. He felt bad because, since they had escaped to B-more, he hadn't been there like he should have. He could no longer afford the luxury of sitting around and catering to Halleigh all day. No longer a major player in the game, he had to rebuild his paper and his operation. That is why he spent so much time in the streets. He just wanted to give his girl and his son the best, but as he watched Halleigh stress herself out, he could see her falling apart at the seams.

"I can't do this," Halleigh whispered. She started getting choked up just thinking about it. She stopped pacing and stared at Malek. "Malek, I need to talk to you. Something happened tonight."

Malek went to her side and wrapped his arms around her as she buried her head in his chest.

"Aye, this is me, Hal. You can tell me anything. It'll be okay."

"Not this time, Malek. I need you to listen to me. I did something really bad tonight—"

Halleigh was ready to put it all out there, but before the confession could fall from her lips, a loud knock at the door interrupted them. It was the middle of the night, and they weren't expecting anyone.

Malek put his hand to his lips to signal for Halleigh to be quiet as he removed his pistol from his waistline. He approached the door and looked out of the peephole. He sighed when he saw it was the detective from the precinct. He handed his gun off to Halleigh, and she put it underneath the couch cushion.

"Who is it?" she whispered.

"It's just that lady cop that helped you out the other night," Malek said.

Halleigh started panicking, and her eyes got as big as saucers. "What! What is she doing here?"

Malek frowned and held out his hand. "I don't know, Hal. Just calm down. She probably forgot to tell you something at the precinct. Chill out." He opened the door and greeted the detective.

"I apologize for the late-night interruption," Detective Rodriguez stated. Halleigh left her bag and identification at the station. I was just returning it."

Halleigh walked toward the door, and Malek stepped to the side. Their son began to cry, and Malek excused himself to take care of him.

Once Rodriguez got Halleigh alone, she stepped in close. "Telling Malek would be a big mistake, Halleigh."

"I wasn't. I told you I was in . . . that I would do it."

Rodriguez reached into Halleigh's jacket pocket and removed the small listening transmitter that she had planted on her before she had left the station. She held it up for Halleigh to see. "This agreement is built on trust, Halleigh. I told you I would be watching you. Everything you do and say, we will know. If this happens again, all deals are off, and I'll take both you and Malek away from your precious little boy. Keep your mouth shut. Stick to the plan. I'll bring your car back to you in the morning."

By the time Malek walked back into the room, Rodriguez had departed, leaving Halleigh feeling even more stuck than before.

Rodriguez pulled out her cell phone and called her partner to update him. "Fuller," she said when he answered, "everything's a go. It shouldn't be long before this Malek kid is out of the picture. The girl's on board."

Halleigh watched out of their window as Rodriguez

left. She wished she had the balls to pull the trigger a third time while she was at it. That way she wouldn't have been in the situation she was in now.

She couldn't believe that Rodriguez had planted a bug on her. If she had done that, there was no telling what other ways she was being monitored. For now, she couldn't tell Malek, but she had to figure something out because their fates were intertwined. Setting up Malek would be like setting herself up because she couldn't see herself without him.

"Hal?" Malek called out.

Halleigh turned around, and just seeing his worried expression melted her heart. He was holding their baby, and it was up to her to make sure that her slipup didn't destroy all three of their lives. If she had just played it smart and cut all of her ties to Flint, then none of this would have ever happened. Her mistake was trusting Tasha. Anyone born and raised in the murder capital of Flint, Michigan was larcenous, and she had risked everything just by inviting her to Baltimore. Their predicament was her fault, and she hated that Malek had to pay for her mistake.

"You good?" he asked.

Despondently, she nodded her head. "Yeah, baby, I'm fine."

"What did you want to tell me?"

"Nothing," she replied, "nothing at all. I'm just shook up, that's all. Let's go to bed."

Chapter Ten

Derek Fuller got an inside tip from one of his snitches on Malek's new spot. That's why he was sitting outside of Malek's establishment and waiting to see if he would show up. Fuller had just left a rendezvous with Scar and found out that all of their spots had been robbed within a matter of twenty-four hours. Fuller instantly knew that Malek was a bigger problem than he thought. He had to take him down if he wanted to keep his stake in Scar's drug business profitable.

"Come on, youngblood. What's taking you so long?" Fuller whispered to himself as he staked out the house and sipped on a cup of coffee.

Scar had requested that Fuller not only shake up Malek's business, but bust him and lock him up. Scar wanted Malek off the streets for good.

Fuller had been posted there for about six hours, and there was no sign of Malek, so he moved to plan B. He picked up his walkie-talkie and let his team know it was time to move in on the spot, although Malek wasn't inside.

"Fuck it! We can't wait on that son of a bitch any longer. Let's move in!" Fuller ordered into the transmitter.

"Roger that, captain," a man said on the other end.

Within seconds, vans whipped onto the block, filling the air with the sound of screeching tires. The side doors slid open on each of the three unmarked vans, and the narcs jumped out with bulletproof vests and their guns drawn, ready for action.

A crew held a battering ram and headed for the front door. On a three count, the police burst through the door, rushing into Malek's crack house. Women were inside cooking coke naked, while cocaine-filled tables and microwaves occupied the spacious studio-style house.

"Everybody on the ground!" Rodriguez grabbed up a girl by the hair when she tried to run to the back door. She yelled, "Don't play with me, dumb bitch!" and flung the girl to the floor by her hair. "Check the back!"

Meanwhile, Fuller drove around the corner, waiting to see if anyone would try to flee from the back of the house, and just as he thought, a man with a duffel bag jumped the gate and tried to get away. Fuller quickly put the pedal to the metal and headed straight for the fleeing man.

As he got closer, he saw it was Dayvid, Malek's little man. "Bingo!" he said, knowing he got a consolation prize by locating Dayvid.

Dayvid saw the car speeding toward him. "Fuck!" He instantly began to put on his best Carl Lewis impersonation and took off full speed.

Fuller quickly whipped behind him and hit him, causing him to fly up in the air and onto the windshield. Fuller stopped, and Dayvid rolled off the car and hit the ground with the bag still in his hands.

Dayvid winced in pain from the extreme back pains the collision caused. "Fuck!" he said as he lay on the ground holding his back.

"Don't move!" Fuller yelled, his gun drawn and pointed directly at Dayvid's head. He snatched the bag and tossed it on the hood of his car. He then flipped Dayvid around and placed handcuffs on him just before patting him down to make sure he didn't have any weapons.

Fuller then stood up and caught his breath. He peeked into the bag and saw nothing but rubber-banded money. "Damn, y'all over there getting it, huh?" he said.

"Fuck you, pig!" Dayvid yelled, showcasing his deep hatred for police.

Fuller chuckled at Dayvid's remark and then gave him a swift kick to the mouth, causing blood to spurt from it instantly.

"I know you. You're Dayvid Porter, right?' Fuller said, already knowing who Dayvid was because he had the whole rundown on Malek's crew. "Where is Malek?" Fuller bent down on one knee and grabbed Dayvid by the back of his neck.

Dayvid ran his tongue across his bloody teeth. "I don't know a Malek."

"Oh, so you want to play games with me?" Fuller nodded his head up and down, getting angrier by the second. He quickly bashed Dayvid's head into the cement, causing a bloody gash to form on his forehead.

Dayvid grimaced in pain, but shortly after, he began to smile, knowing he was getting under Fuller's skin by not giving up Malek's whereabouts.

"You can give your man up and tell me where he is, or go down to the station. It's all on you!" Fuller yelled as he began to grip tighter around the back of Dayvid's neck.

"I ain't telling you shit!" Dayvid spat out more blood.

Fuller had had enough and realized that Dayvid was loyal to Malek. "We will see how loyal you are." He yanked Dayvid off the ground and stuffed him into the back seat. They were about to take a little ride down to the station.

Fuller had Dayvid in a chair in the middle of the interrogation room of the police precinct. "You're looking at three to five, Dayvid." He rested both of his hands on the cold steel table. "You were maintaining a drug house, and I found thirty grand in your possession."

Fuller was itching to get Malek in the worst way, but Dayvid wasn't budging. He had a clean record, and he knew that he would only get a slap on a wrist for what Fuller was trying to pin him with.

Fuller continued to circle around the youngster. "Just give Malek up, and you can go scot-free. I will forget about what I found on you, and it would be as if you were never there."

"I don't know a Malek." Dayvid grinned. He would never in a million years cross his big homie. Never. He began to block out all Fuller was saying and began to think back to the first time he'd met Malek.

***

Dayvid sat sunken low in the tinted Grand Am, watching Malek closely. "I'm about to take all of that shit," he whispered to himself as he gripped the all-black .357 handgun. He had a ski mask rolled on the top of his head and was waiting for the right moment to ambush Malek.

Dayvid had been following him for days, and he was waiting until Malek led him straight to his home, because Dayvid thought that was where he most likely kept his stash. Dayvid needed that money in the worst way. The city was dry, and he was hungry. He had been watching Malek closely and knew he was an out-of-towner that came to B-more moving coke.

Dayvid had trailed Malek as he stopped at five different crack houses. It was the first of the month, so he knew Malek was picking up his trap from his spots. In Dayvid's eyes, that day was the perfect day to rob him.

The sun was just setting as Dayvid followed Malek to a nice-sized brick house.

"This must be where the nigga stay," Dayvid said to himself, as he witnessed Malek pull into the driveway and hop out of his car with the duffel bag in hand.

Dayvid was parked about a half a block down, but he still had a clear view of Malek getting out of the car. He made sure his gun was locked and loaded and got out of his car as soon as he saw Malek enter the home. There were no more cars in the driveway or on the curb, so he assumed Malek was there alone.

"He must be about to go count or stash the money inside," Dayvid said as he crept to the back of the house.

Dayvid's young mind didn't think logically, and he didn't care what he was getting himself into. He just knew Malek was getting money, and he wanted a piece of it.

He crept to the back, where there was a swimming pool and a glass patio. He quickly dipped into the back patio and saw the sliding double doors that led into the home. He slowly approached the double doors and glanced into the home, to see if the coast was clear.

After a few seconds of observing, Dayvid pulled out a lockpick, but when he gently slid the door, he noticed it was unlocked. *Hell yeah,* he thought to himself. It was his lucky day, and everything was going perfect.

He slowly stepped around the kitchen's porcelain counter and heard the sound of a money counter purring. Malek had to be dealing with big paper, a stickup kid's dream. He smiled as he pulled down his ski mask, thinking about how much paper he was about to get.

Dayvid crept to the room with his gun in hand. He saw Malek at the table with his back turned toward him, putting the money in rubber bands as it came out of the machine. He slowly and carefully snuck up behind Malek, his gun pointed directly at Malek's head.

The money machine stopped, and the room grew quiet as Malek paused.

Without even turning around to face Dayvid, Malek said without an ounce of fear in his heart or shakiness in his voice, "I was wondering what was taking you so long."

What the fuck? Dayvid thought to himself. He wondered how Malek knew he was sneaking up behind him. "Come up off all of that dough, homeboy," he yelled, his hand shaking nervously.

"You sure you want to do this, young nigga?" Malek carefully swung around in his chair, so he could look the young robber in his eyes.

"Fuck all the talking, nigga! Put the money in the bag!" Dayvid said, avoiding eye contact with Malek.

"Look, you have two choices. You can rob me of this money and then deal with the consequences of taking money from a nigga like me." Malek folded his hands together. "Or you can put that gun down, and I will give you a job. I will let you work for me and show you how to get money rather than take it.

"One thing about robbing, once your stolen money is gone, you're right back to square one and broke again. But if you learn how to get money, you will never be broke." Malek looked the youngster straight in the eye and recognized the fear within them.

Malek's logic made a lot of sense to Dayvid, who wanted to get out of the robbing business desperately and get into the hustle game. He had always fantasized about moving up in the ranks and becoming a kingpin, so Malek's offer was very tempting. But the possibility of Malek just talking to get out of the situation had him hesitant.

"How do I know if I put the gun down, you won't try to kill me?"

"You are just going to have to trust me."

Malek spoke with a supreme calmness that had Dayvid petrified. All of Dayvid's instincts told him to just rob Malek and turn down the offer, but his heart told him otherwise. He used his free hand to pull his ski mask to the top of his head, and then he lowered his gun.

Malek instantly knew he had accepted his offer. "Good choice, youngblood." He turned around and began to rubber-band the money.

Dayvid stood there confused, as he didn't know what to do next.

Malek finally spoke up after a few seconds of silence. "Believe me, you made the right choice," he said. "I want you to take a look behind you."

Dayvid frowned his face up, not knowing what Malek was getting to. Dayvid did as he was told, and when he turned around, his heart almost dropped to the floor. There was a man standing there with a Mossberg pump aimed directly at his chest. Dayvid flinched as he looked down at the steel that was now pressed against his chest.

"I knew you were coming. I saw you from a mile away. If you had tried to rob me, karma would have come instantly, and my man would've blown your brains out. But I respect your bravery, and I'ma keep my word." Malek pulled out the chair from underneath the table for Dayvid. "Have a seat."

The man holding the shotgun lowered his weapon, and Dayvid joined Malek at the table. That was the beginning of a relationship that would become closer than close. Since that day, Malek and Dayvid had become inseparable, and Malek showed his youngster how to get to the monster, molding him to be Baltimore's next kingpin.

***

Dayvid snapped out of his dream and focused on the present.

Fuller was right in his face with an intense stare. "So what's it going to be? The ball is in your court." He waited for a response from the young Dayvid.

"Suck my dick!" Dayvid calmly said, looking through Fuller as if he weren't even there. Dayvid wasn't going to roll on his man.

Fuller became enraged, knowing that Dayvid was young and also that as a first-time offender, would get just a slap on the wrist, and that only infuriated him even more. He gave Dayvid a swift jab to the eye, for good measure, and stormed out of the room.

Dayvid took the punch like a man, and after the stars wore off, he thought about what Malek had taught him: stay loyal, which was exactly what he'd just done.

Within twenty-four hours, Malek was waiting for Dayvid outside of the jailhouse in a tinted car. He had sent his attorney in to bail Dayvid out, and just like that, he was on the streets again.

Malek's attorney had discovered that Fuller had raided the house without a warrant, so all the paraphernalia and evidence was inadmissible. Malek would just move his spot and would be open for business by the end of the day. Scar had his work cut out for him because Malek wasn't an amateur.

"What's up, kid?" Malek said as Dayvid entered the

car along with one of Malek's workers that he'd sent in for him. A smiling Malek blew his horn at the attorney, who was getting into his vehicle across the parking lot. He knew he had outwitted Scar.

"What up, Malek? I'm glad to be out of that stink-hole." Dayvid got comfortable in the front seat and leaned back.

"Yeah. Tell me about it." Malek then reached over and playfully smacked Dayvid on the head. "You did good, you did good," and with that, he pulled off smiling.

Malek had his own little plan for Scar. It was obvious the man didn't know how he got down, and Malek fully planned on showing him.

Chapter Eleven

As Halleigh watched Malek sleep, she cried. There was no way she could stay in his life. After everything, their end had finally come. She leaned down and kissed his lips. He was a heavy sleeper, so he didn't stir.

"I love you, Malek," she said as she arose from their bed. She couldn't stop staring at him. Even though she knew she could never forget one detail about him, she wanted to burn his image in her brain because this was the last time she would ever see him again. She had to put distance between them. She had become a liability and was doing what was best for everyone involved by disappearing.

If Rodriguez knew she planned on skipping town, the shit would hit the fan, but by the time anyone realized she was gone, it would be too late. All she had to do was make sure that no one saw her leave and that she wasn't followed.

She pulled a suitcase from the closet, moving as quietly as possible, and began to pack some of her things. She didn't need much. A few clothes would do. She then went into Malek's petty cash stash and clipped five Gs from it. She had never stolen a thing from him in her life, but she needed this. Five thousand dollars was going to buy her a way out of town and hopefully be enough for her to start a new life.

She went into her son's nursery and checked on him. The last thing she wanted was to walk out of her baby's life, but she couldn't take him with her. She just hoped that one day he would understand, that both her child and Malek would understand. She kissed her fingers and placed them on his forehead then left the room.

She penned a note before she left because she would be ceasing all forms of communication. She didn't even want to take her cell phone with her because she knew she could be tracked down if she did.

Dear Malek,

I love you and have always loved you. I know that I always will, and because I love you so much, I have to leave you. I know you will never understand why I am doing this, but I need you to trust me the same way I have always trusted you. I'm doing this for our family because, even though we all won't be together, it is the only way to keep all of us safe. Don't forget about me, Malek, and please don't let our son. Tell him every day that I love him. Tell yourself that every day. I will always be thinking about you. I will never move on, and I will never forget what we have.

You were made for me, Malek. We both made a lot of mistakes over the years that caused us to stay apart. This is just one more of them, but you will always have my heart. Raise our son right, Malek. He needs you, and you can't be there for him if you're in the streets. I don't want him to end

up like us. I don't want him to have to see what we've seen.
We've been to hell and back. Protect him. Open your eyes,
Malek, and watch those who are watching you. You are all
he has. I love you.
   Always Yours,
   Halleigh

She placed the letter on her pillow, knowing he would
find it when he awoke, and then reluctantly she walked
out on the people she loved the most.

Halleigh peered out onto the street. There were always cars sitting on the block at night, but tonight they
all looked suspicious. Rodriguez had said that the police
would always be watching, so to be safe, Halleigh went
out of the back of the building.

Creeping like a cat through the back alley, she walked
until she was on the next block and then ran until she
was able to catch a cab in the early morning hours.

"Where to?" the cab driver asked.

"BWI," she stated. She never looked back as the cab
pulled off, afraid that if she did, she may not go through
with her plan.

Malek awoke the next day to the sound of his son crying. He was used to Halleigh waking up with him, so he
wasn't used to all of the screaming.

"Hal? Baby girl?" he called out from underneath the
sheets.

When she didn't respond, he sat up. She never let their
son cry for too long.

He got up and walked into their son's nursery. "Hey, li'l man. What you crying for?" he asked as he picked him up, and his crying stopped instantly. "Where's your mommy?"

Malek went into their living room and saw that Halleigh wasn't there either. She never left the house without telling him her plans, so he found her absence odd. "Hal!" he yelled, but she was nowhere to be found.

He didn't begin to worry until he called her cell phone and heard it ringing inside of their house. Malek followed the ringing of the phone, which led him back to their bedroom. Her phone was on the nightstand on her side of the bed, and as he sat down, he noticed the letter she left behind.

With his son in his arms, he picked up the note and read it. Malek had never been an emotional young man. His mentor, Jamaica Joe, had hardened him long ago, but reading the good-bye letter that Halleigh had left for him broke him down. Tears accumulated in his eyes as he gripped his son tight. He wasn't ashamed to cry.

Losing a woman like Halleigh would break any man. He loved her endlessly, unconditionally, and couldn't believe this was happening. His heart felt broken. He had never felt this much pain. When they had been separated before, it didn't hurt this bad because other people had kept them away from one another in the past. This time Halleigh had chosen to leave him.

She left me, Malek thought in anguish. He didn't understand.

For so long they had fought to be with each other,

and now she had packed her bags and given up on them. He couldn't help but feel like this was his fault. He had made a lot of bad decisions, and he hadn't kept her safe over the years. He thought maybe she was beginning to regret all of the heartache she had suffered just to be his girl.

She ain't the only one who gave up something for us to be together, he thought.

Malek remembered his dreams of being a hoop star. They had been completely realistic until that fateful night so many years ago had changed the game plan for them both. The night Halleigh was raped had changed the course of their lives forever, and because he loved her, he had given up everything to try to protect her. But through it all, he never blamed her. He simply let go of the past and focused on what he had, which was Halleigh, instead of what he could have had.

A knock at the door caused Malek to gain hope. *Maybe Halleigh has come back.* He stood and raced to the door, practically snatching it off the hinges as he opened it. Disappointment filled him when he saw Detective Rodriguez.

"Now is not a good time, detective," he said.

"Well, then I won't take up much of it. I came to return Halleigh's vehicle. We located it on the south end of town. Whoever mugged her left it in an abandoned parking lot," Rodriguez said as she held out the keys for Malek. "Is Halleigh home? I would like to speak with her for a minute."

"Halleigh's not here."

"Is there a better time for me to stop back?" Rodriguez pushed. *Where the hell did she go? I had a car sitting on the building all night,* she thought angrily. She had a gut feeling that Halleigh had run, and she was infuriated.

"I got her keys. There really isn't a need for you to stop back," Malek replied. He began to close the door. He hated the police, and his patience with her had expired. He had more pressing issues on his mind.

"I have a few more questions for her," Rodriguez insisted.

Malek sighed. "She has your card. If I see her, I will have her contact you." He shut the door in her face.

Rodriguez stormed out of the building and immediately put in the call to her partner, Derek Fuller. Without a vehicle, there were only a few ways out of town, so she put a police detail on every bus station, airport, and train station in the city. There was no way she was going to let Halleigh escape. She would call out the entire Narcotics Unit of Baltimore before she let Halleigh slip through her fingers.

Malek's suspicion was aroused by the detective's interest in Halleigh. She seemed to be too persistent in her effort to speak with Halleigh. Her sudden disappearance didn't make sense, but his gut was telling him that this lady cop had something to do with it.

That was the only thing he could attribute Halleigh's sudden change of heart to. They hadn't been having problems; in fact, he, had never loved Halleigh more. After almost losing her back in Flint, he cherished every moment that he spent with her now, and he knew that she felt the same.

Something is up, he thought, now sure of himself that Halleigh needed his help.

Something was nagging at him. He returned to his bedroom and read her letter again, trying to read between the lines.

One line of her letter stuck out to him the most. "Watch those who are watching you," he whispered as her warning jumped out on the paper.

And like a light bulb coming on in his head, he thought, *The cops are watching.* He rushed into the hallway and down to the window that peered out over the street.

For the first time, he noticed the unmarked squad car that was hawking his building. *Fuck!* He cursed himself. *How long have they been on me? What the fuck they watching me for? A nigga ain't moving bricks. And how long has Halleigh known? What do they have over her that will make her skip town?*

Malek was beginning to think that more had happened that night than a carjacking, and as he raced back to his apartment, he tried to figure out where Halleigh had gone. *Think like her. Where would she go?*

Halleigh sat in the airport eagerly and nervously waiting for the delayed flights to resume service. She didn't have time for this. A security breach had caused the entire airport to shut down, and she had been waiting for hours for them to resume ticket sales. She figured that Malek had gotten her letter by now, and she was wondering how he had reacted. She wished she could go back home and make everything nice, but it was a wrap for her life in Baltimore.

As soon as she was able to, she was purchasing a one-way ticket out of the city. She figured she would go down south to North Carolina, where her mother was from and where her grandmother still lived. Even though Halleigh had never met the woman, she knew her name, and was hoping they could get acquainted once she arrived. If not, then she would just have to do what she did best: survive.

At least down there she would be out of hot water. *Maybe one day I can come back for my son,* she thought.

She felt herself becoming emotional at the thought of everything she was leaving behind. She went to use the restroom. Her eyes were red and puffy. She looked a hot mess. She couldn't wait to get out of Baltimore, so she could have peace of mind.

As she emerged from the bathroom, she looked toward the front counter. Her heart skipped a beat when she saw Rodriguez questioning one of the airline employees. Halleigh automatically knew that this was no coincidence. She was there looking for her. She knew that if Rodriguez was there, it was a good possibility that more cops were on the scene as well.

Halleigh quickly ducked back into the restroom. Creating a commotion at the airport was the last thing she wanted to do, but she had to get out of there. She peeked out of the door, and while Rodriguez was distracted at the ticket counter, she slowly eased out, keeping her head low to remain inconspicuous. Walking as quickly as possible out of the airport, when she finally emerged outside, she ran to the first cab she saw.

"Hal!"

She stopped mid-step and looked up in disbelief when she heard Malek calling her name. She had one foot inside of the cab as she saw him pulling up behind her, blowing his horn urgently to get her attention. Shocked, her mouth dropped open in surprise.

"Get in, Halleigh!" he shouted.

She rushed over to his car and jumped inside. She ducked low, keeping her eyes on the side mirrors.

Just as Malek pulled away, Halleigh saw Rodriguez emerge from the airport. "Go! Go!" she yelled.

When she was sure they were out of any police radar, she sat up in her seat. Her son was crying from his car seat in the back, and his cries affected her, causing her tears to flow too.

"You wanna tell me what's going on now, Halleigh?"

"How did you find me?"

"I know you, Hal," he said as he drove with one hand and touched her chin gently with the other. "You are me, ma. You ran, and I knew you wasn't riding no bus or train. You think you're too good for that." He smiled mockingly.

She shook her head and wiped her eyes. "You should have let me go, Malek," she said softly. "You don't know what's going on."

"Then why don't you tell me? I know the cops are watching me. Your letter told me that. But what is it that you are not telling me? We're better than this, Halleigh. Your burden is supposed to be my burden."

"I'll tell you everything. Can we just go somewhere, to a hotel room or something, so I can get my head together? Then we'll talk, and I'll tell you everything."

Malek and Halleigh checked into the Courtyard Marriot in Linthicum, and once they were safely inside with their child, it was time for her to fess up. Malek waited patiently for her to find her words.

"You can tell me, Halleigh. Whatever it is, just say it."

"I fucked up," she began. "When we first came here, you told me over and over again to let the past go. You told me that everything and everyone in Flint were dead to us, but I didn't listen. With you in the streets all the time, I felt like I had nobody to talk to, no friends, no real life in Baltimore. So I called Tasha." She paused to see what Malek would say, but he remained silent. His facial expression was blank, so Halleigh couldn't read his emotions.

"Keep going," he said.

"I invited Tasha to come to Baltimore about a week ago, and we met for lunch downtown. I thought she was my friend, Malek. I would have never told her where we were if I ever thought she would put us in jeopardy."

"Stop talking in circles, Hal. Just tell me," he stated seriously.

"She came to town, but she brought Toy with her. They followed me from the restaurant, but I shook them."

Malek closed his eyes because he remembered Halleigh had specifically tried to tell him that someone had followed her, but he thought she was paranoid and over-reacting.

"That next night they followed me from my job, and I refused to lead them back to you and the baby, so I just pulled over. I found an abandoned lot and I got out. I had started carrying one of your guns because I was ter-rified. I've been terrified since the day we got here, but I was tired of running, tired of being followed. I was tired of being the victim. They tried to get me to lead them to you. I refused, and Toy hit me. I just reacted and I shot her, Malek. I killed her, and then I killed Tasha for set-ting me up."

"And the cop saw it," Malek finished, putting two and two together.

Halleigh nodded. "She saw everything. She said if I didn't help her get you, then she would throw me in prison for the rest of my life. I could never bring myself to harm you, but I can't go to jail either, Malek. So I ran. I just thought if I got as far away from here as possible, it would fix things."

"Come here, ma," he said as he pulled her onto the bed he was sitting on. He wiped her tears away. He could only imagine how Halleigh felt. Having taken many lives himself, he knew Halleigh wasn't built for murder.

She broke down in his arms. "What am I going to do?" she asked.

"You're going to do exactly what they want you to do. You're going to cooperate with the police," he said in a low but sure tone.

"What?" She looked up at him in confusion. "Malek, they'll throw you in jail."

"Look at that little boy over there," he said, pointing to their son. "He needs you, Halleigh. You're his mother. You didn't ask for any of this. You just took on the role of being with me. I would never make you pay for that. I love you too much to ever see something bad happen to you. I can handle whatever the cops have coming my way. You just promise me that you'll always take care of my son."

Halleigh was hysterical crying and snot running down her nose. "I can't, Malek. I can't do that to you. This isn't supposed to be how we end. I need you."

"And I need you, Hal. I need you to be strong, baby girl. You're my world, and I need you to trust me. This is the only way. I'm a man, and I can stand behind all of the decisions I've made in my life, but before I let them take me, I need to know that you can hold things down for me while I'm away."

She nodded as he held her face. "I will try for you, Malek. I will do whatever you need me to do."

"I've got some money put up. It's not a lot, but it's enough for you and the baby to live for a couple years. Nothing extravagant, but it will pay for rent and food for a while until you can get on your feet."

"I don't want to do this, Malek."

"You have to, Halleigh."

As Malek schooled Halleigh on how to survive without him, she almost tuned him out. She didn't want to believe this was happening, but this was real and there was no avoiding the inevitable. She was grateful she had a man like Malek, who was willing to take responsibility for the situation, but it didn't stop the sadness that plagued her.

Chapter Twelve

So many thoughts went through Malek's head as he drove down the highway along with Dayvid. They were just getting back from visiting the coke connect, and Dayvid was officially plugged. Malek had introduced him to the "birdman" and put him in a position of power, just as his deceased mentor, Jamaica Joe, had done for Malek when he was younger.

He kept visualizing Halleigh's face when she told him Rodriguez was blackmailing her. The hurt in her eyes was like daggers to his heart. He never second-guessed his decision to give himself up for his girl's freedom. He knew that when he walked in his own house it could be wired, starting off a domino effect that would land him in jail for a very long time.

Malek's heart began to ache as he thought about his son growing up without him. Nevertheless, it was better than his son growing up without both mother and father. He'd always told Halleigh that he would keep her out of harm's way when they relocated to Baltimore, but he'd failed to do that, and the guilt was weighing heavy on his soul.

"Remember everything I have taught you," Malek

preached to his protégé. "You are too smart to stay in this game long enough for it to consume you. Don't be like me and let the allure of the money keep you in. Make money and exit. That's the key. Timing is everything."

Dayvid just sat back and listened closely as Malek hit him with a few last words of encouragement and instructions.

Malek dropped Dayvid off to his block and watched as he exited the car. He grabbed him just before he got completely out and hugged him tight.

Dayvid was confused and didn't know why Malek was acting so funny.

"I love you, my nigga," Malek said as he held on to Dayvid for a couple of extra seconds.

"Love you too. What's up, nigga? Why you acting all different?"

Malek released him. "Don't worry about it. Just be safe out here, all right? And one more thing."

"What's up?" Dayvid looked at Malek dead in the eyes.

"If I'm not around, I want you to look after my son and Halleigh just as I did for you." Malek looked forward, avoiding eye contact with Dayvid.

"I got you," Dayvid said as he exited the car.

Dayvid was taken off guard by Malek's comments, but he decided not to say anything about it. He noticed that Malek seemed to be stressing lately, and decided to address it at a later time.

Just before Malek pulled off, he caught a glimpse of the pinky ring he had given Dayvid and smirked. He knew Dayvid would hold it down in the streets and carry on his legacy properly. With that thought, Malek smiled and pulled off, headed home.

Malek knew that the next time he talked to Halleigh, she would be wearing a wire, and he would have to incriminate himself to get her off the hook for murder. He prepared himself mentally as he was about to voluntarily walk the path of self-destruction.

Halleigh sat in the unmarked van on her block, three houses down from her and Malek's home. She clenched her jaws tight, and water filled her eyes as Rodriguez put the wire on her. She was shirtless, with nothing on but a bra, as Rodriguez applied tape on her chest to position the microphone right.

"Nice rack," Fuller said as he stared at Halleigh's plump breasts.

"Fuck you!" Halleigh said as she gave him a cold stare. If looks could kill, Fuller would have been circled in chalk.

"You wish," Fuller said with a sinister grin. "Look, you have to get him to say something about him supplying kilos of dope to his runners. If he doesn't say that, the deal is off."

"I know what the fuck I have to do! I hate you!" Halleigh said as she continued to give Fuller a deadly stare.

"Yeah, yeah. Just remember what I said. If you don't follow through with this, you will never see your son, except through steel bars. It's your choice."

Halleigh knew Malek was sacrificing himself for his family, and the fact that she was about to help Fuller put him behind bars made her sick to her stomach. She had left Malek Jr. with a babysitter, not wanting him to be around when this disaster went down.

"Okay, you're done," Rodriguez said as she tapped the microphone to make sure it was on.

Halleigh snatched her shirt from the seat and began to put it on, shaking her head from side to side. She knew the countdown to Malek's demise had begun. If she had to sacrifice herself for Malek, she would have. But Malek Jr.'s well-being was at risk. So, with the permission of her man, she had to do what she had to do. It was show time.

Halleigh stepped out of the van and slammed the door as hard as she could. As she walked to her house, so many different emotions began to run through her body as she felt the burden of the situation weighing heavy on her soul—hatred for Fuller, and guilt for herself.

"How did I get myself into this shit?" she whispered as she entered her house and waited for Malek.

Malek pulled up to his home and turned off the ignition. He took a deep breath and prepared for what was ahead. He was determined for his son to have a normal life and not have to go through the hardships that he himself had encountered. And to do that, he had to give himself to the law.

He stepped out of the car and glanced down the street. He noticed two vans with plumbing advertisements. He already knew the vans held policemen waiting to move in on him. He quickly focused on his house and headed that way.

"Hey, baby," he yelled as he stepped through the door. "I'm home!"

Halleigh appeared from the back with tears in her eyes and her hands over her mouth, trying to stop from crying aloud. She ran into his arms, and he embraced her tight.

Malek kissed her on her neck. In the lowest tone he could muster, he whispered in her ear, "I love you, Halleigh. Always have and always will. Let's get this over with, okay." He stepped back from her.

Halleigh let her tears flow freely down her cheeks as she nodded her head in agreement.

As soon as Malek nodded his head, giving her the green light to start the rehearsed conversation, she did.

"Malek, you have to stop selling drugs. I'm tired of this life," she said just as he had instructed her to the night before. Halleigh's voice began to crack, and she ran her fingers through her hair in frustration. She mouthed silently to Malek, "I can't do this."

But he smiled at her and put his hand on her shoulder, helping her through it. "I have to flip a couple more kilos, and then I'm done," he said. "My dope connect, Scar, wouldn't like if I just stopped buying from him. It's not that simple." Malek smiled inside, knowing he had just incriminated Scar by saying his name. If he was going to go out, he was going out with a bang.

***

Detective Fuller sat in the van, earphones on, listening to their every word. He chuckled to himself at Malek's remark about Scar.

"That nigga think he's slick," Fuller said to himself. He immediately thought about how he would edit that small portion out of the wiretap before turning it in as evidence.

Fuller was patiently waiting for the right time to rush in with his squad and put Malek in handcuffs. He looked down at the duffel bag that contained four kilos and stepped-on cocaine that he would eventually pin on Malek. With the drugs and the wiretaps indicating that he was a heavy drug supplier, Malek was sure to spend a long time behind bars.

Scar's money had slowed up drastically, which meant that Fuller had seen his cut from the drug business slow up too, and he wasn't having it. Fuller wanted Malek off the streets just as bad as Scar wanted him off the streets.

"Come on, Malek, tell on yourself a little bit more."

"I just hit my spot off with a kilo a piece." Malek clenched his teeth tight, knowing he was telling on himself. But when he thought about what he was doing it for, he had no problem with doing so. Malek would tell on himself a thousand times and serve a million years, if it meant that his son would have a good life and Halleigh stayed free.

Halleigh cried as she stood there looking into Malek's eyes.

Malek had said enough to satisfy the police, so he grabbed and hugged his woman and kissed her. "I love you with all my heart, and you are the love of my life."

"I love you too, Malek." Halleigh gripped him tight and buried her face into his chiseled chest. She tiptoed and whispered in his ear, "Let's just leave town. Let's run," trying to exhaust every possible option to change the inevitable.

Malek quickly shook his head no. He would've considered it if they didn't have a baby to bring along, but he knew that being on the run with a baby was immoral. He couldn't bring himself to have his son caught up in the web of the treacherous street life he had created.

"I'm tired of running, Hal. I got us into this, I'ma get us out." He looked deep into Halleigh's eyes and added, "Tell my son that I will always love him."

Those words broke Halleigh's heart, knowing that Malek wouldn't be able to tell Malek Jr. that himself without being behind bars.

Malek pulled his gun from his waist and placed his other hand on Halleigh's cheek. It was the most difficult thing either of them ever had to do.

"We will be together again," he said.

Malek flashed back to years ago when they'd first met in high school. He thought back to a time when she was pure and innocent. He would trade his life to give Halleigh back her innocence. The ills of their hometown Flint had forced them to move to Baltimore, and even there, trouble found them.

He walked out of the door with gun in hand. "Bye, Halleigh," he said.

Halleigh saw the look in Malek's eyes, the pain that was embedded deep within. She didn't fully understand what that pained look meant, but she would soon find out.

Scar sat back smoking a kush-filled cigar and thought about how business would pick up, now that Malek was on the road of destruction. Fuller had just phoned him and let him know that the master plan was in motion, and that Malek would be behind bars before the night's end.

Scar already had his goons in place to rush Malek's block and give his old workers an ultimatum: Get down or lay down. He had just checkmated Malek after a long battle of mental chess. The only thing left to do now was to wait for Fuller's call to confirm the arrest.

"Victory feels so good," Scar said as he watched the young lady go up and down on his shaft, making it disappear and reappear over and over again. "Damn, Mrs. Fuller, that feels good," he crooned as his toes began to curl.

He looked at her shapely naked body and admired her smooth skin while she pleased him. He reached over and smacked her buttocks, making a small wave flow, enticing him even more. The view was mesmerizing and made his pipe even harder.

While Scar's partner was handling business for him, he was banging out Fuller's wife. Scar, at that point, felt on top of the world. He had a dime piece sucking him off, bringing him to the brink of an orgasm, while his main rival was about to be nonexistent, making him the king of Baltimore.

"Move in! He's coming out of the house," Fuller yelled into the phone. He smiled. He was about to lock Malek up for a very long time. He was satisfied with the recordings he had and was ready to snatch Malek up.

Fuller looked closer at Malek stepping off of the porch and noticed that he had a gun in hand. "He has a gun!" Fuller screamed into the walkie-talkie as Rodriguez slid the van's door open.

Fuller's squad had already rushed Malek with their guns drawn, but Malek had his gun drawn also and pointed at the oncoming crew. Fuller jumped out of the van along with Rodriguez, their guns out.

"Drop the fucking gun!" one of policemen said as they slowly approached Malek.

"You drop yo' mufuckin' gun! I'm not putting down shit!" Malek yelled as he pointed his gun at each officer.

Fuller cautiously approached his crew and put his red beam on Malek's chest, ready to blast at any sudden movement by Malek.

Malek gripped his gun tight. He had no intentions of going to jail that day. He had planned to go out blazing, just like Jamaica Joe would have. Malek was about to go out like a gangster, no doubt.

Fuller closed one eye and aimed straight for Malek's head. "Drop that gun! You don't want to do this!"

"Fuck you!" Malek screamed, spit flying out of his

mouth. His trigger finger began to itch. He saw Fuller's face and locked his aim on him, feeling deep hatred for him. The cops had blackmailed his girl and caused all of the pandemonium. He hated him deep down in his soul. The more he thought about leaving Halleigh and his son, he grew more irate.

A single tear dropped from Malek's left eye—a tear not of sadness, but of pain. "I'm from Flint, Michigan, mufucka!" Malek's grip grew even tighter, his index finger resting on the trigger. "Do y'all know who the fuck I am? Huh? I'm cut from the cloth of Jamaica Joe! Fuck all y'all!" Malek screamed, ten guns pointed at him.

"Malek! No!" Halleigh yelled as she stepped out of the door. Her heart dropped as she saw the police standing in front of the love of her life.

As Halleigh stepped off the porch trying to get to Malek, he looked back, and that quick movement by him made Fuller fire a shot at him.

That started a chain reaction among the other narcs, and the bullets started flying one after another, hitting Malek in the chest, jerking him from left to right.

As Malek lay there dying, all Halleigh could think of was that not only did she just lose the love of her life, but it was the end of an era.

Exerpt From Baltimore Chronicles

Chapter 1

The Take Down

Detective Derek Fuller splashed water on his face, took a deep breath and looked up at himself in the small, dull mirror that hung in the men's bathroom inside the station house. He noticed the bags that were starting to form under his eyes, but he knew those came with the territory. Fighting against the Maryland drug trade was not an easy win. Shaking off his jitters, Derek stared at himself. He thought that despite those bags, all his smooth cinnamon colored skin, and chestnut brown eyes still made him a fine ass dude.

Refocusing, Derek spoke to himself, "Let's get it nigga. This ain't no time to have second thoughts," he checked his gear, shifted his bulletproof vest and shrugged into his raid jacket. It was six o'clock in the morning and he had to get into the right state of mind for the task at hand. Walking back out into the squad room he put his game face on.

"I hope everybody is ready for Scar. Let's fuckin' roll and take this nigga out. This mu'fucka only thinks he is the leader of the bitch-ass dirty money crew," Derek announced to the four officers that comprised his unit. They all stood at attention and started gathering their battle gear. "Yo, Fuller . . . can I bring this baby with me?" Officer Rodriguez asked, picking up the brand new MP-5 they had just acquired. The big weapon looked out of place in the petite woman's hands. To the average eye she would appear weak and out of her element, but Fuller had come up in the academy with Rodriguez and knew never to underestimate her. She had the gumption that most men never mustered and she was an asset to his team. He trusted Rodriguez with his life and in the game they played that meant a lot. She never hesitated to pull a trigger and if he was the first man through the door, she was always right behind him.

"Damn straight," Derek replied, flashing his perfect smile and leading his unit out the door.

Derek felt powerful in his new position as lead Detective of the Drug Enforcement Section of the Division I of the Maryland State Troopers. Living and working in the roughest part of Baltimore, Maryland; Derek had put in work, moving up from a car chasing, ticket giving state trooper to a narcotics street officer and now leader of his own narcotics interdiction unit. Derek knew all about the so-called "Dirty Money Crew" and their notorious leader, Stephon "Scar" Johnson. Everyone in the Baltimore area knew about Scar and his powerful drug ring. He ran cocaine up and down the interstate with ease. On top of that he was a jack-of-all trades. He had his hand in everything from extortion and illegal gambling to prostitution. If there was money to be made in the underworld of B-more than Scar was getting it. Scar had been reigning terror on the streets for years now. He was considered the Rayful Edmunds of Baltimore. Only difference was he didn't get caught. He deemed himself untouchable and moved like a ghost through the streets; getting money but going unseen most of the time. Rumor had it that on his climb to the top, Scar had taken out ten police officers and two Government officials. But with no proof and witnesses that always turned up dead or missing, it had been an almost impossible undertaking for the overmatched and undermanned state troopers to touch Scar. That did not stop Derek from pursuing Scar. Having been born in the inner city of Baltimore Derek knew a little about the streets. He was also aware of what he needed to do to prove himself to his bosses and the crime syndicates in the streets. His success as head of the D.E.S. depended on the attention he would receive for taking Scar down.

As Derek and his unit arrived at their destination in the worst hood in Baltimore, Derek shook his head and smiled. It was just like his confidential informant had told him; Scar was making a very rare early morning creep appearance at one of his most lucrative trap houses. When Derek noticed Scar's tricked out black Escalade, complete with its candy paint job, parked on the side of the trap house, Derek felt his dick jump in his pants. He was that excited by this opportunity to shine.

"Here we fuckin' go!" Derek mumbled under his breath, geeking himself up for the task at hand. His heart was beating so fast that it threatened to jump out of his chest. Yanking his glock out of his hip holster, Derek barely put his vehicle in park before he swung the door open and jumped out. He waved his hands over his head, placed his fingers up to his lips and made a fist signaling his unit to get into their rehearsed raid positions. They all silently exited their black Impalas. Ducking low they fell in line one behind the other and stacked on the door. Derek was first in the stack—he would announce their arrival. The ram holder stood on the opposite side of the door and the rest of the unit knew their roles in bringing up the back of the stack. Derek raised his right hand and silently counted down. Three, two, one . . . at that the ram holder sent the heavy duty metal crashing into the shabby plywood door. The wood splintered open with one hit. Inside, bodies began scrambling in all directions.

"Police! Police! Put ya fuckin' hands up now!" Derek screamed, waving his weapon back and forth, pointing it at all of Scar's scrambling workers for emphasis. All of the members of the D.E.S. trampled inside, grabbing whomever they could and tossing them to the ground. Derek continued into the house with his gun drawn and keeping his back close to the walls. He had his eye on the prize and he was not going to stop until he had it in custody. Derek came to a closed door at the back of the house. With his gun trained on the door he kicked it open.

"Damn man, put the gun down. You ain't gotta go

all hard and shit," Scar said calmly as he exhaled a cigar smoke ring in front of him, poisoning the air surrounding Damon. Derek was baffled as he stared into Scar's ugly, hard line, and scarred face. It was like Scar knew they were coming. He didn't even flinch when the door came crashing in around him.

"Put your fucking hands up mu'fucka!" Derek screamed, pointing his gun right at Scar's head. "Now! Show me your hands!"

"A'ight, a'ight. Calm down cowboy," Scar said, smirking and stubbing out his cigar on the table he sat behind. Derek was getting more pissed by the minute. He was looking a little silly in front of his unit while Scar was looking cool, calm and collected. "They pay you to act all extra?" Scar asked, still smiling.

"Let's go! Stand the fuck up nigga!" Derek barked again.

"I got one better for you. I will put my hands out so you can cuff me," Scar chuckled, his smile causing his severely disfigured charcoal colored face to contort into a monstrous mug. Pushing away from the table Scar lifted his six foot, three inch, gorilla frame up from the chair. Laughing like he had heard a joke, Scar turned around and assumed the handcuffing position. Scar's nonchalant attitude pissed Derek off. How dare he act as if he had the upper hand.

"Cuff this son of a bitch!" Derek spat as one of his officer's moved in swiftly to lock the cuffs on Scar's thick wrists.

"Son of a bitch? Ain't that the pot calling the kettle black," Scar replied, still laughing.

Derek grabbed the cuffs roughly making sure he clamped them extra tight so the metal would cut into Scar's skin. Derek led Scar out of the house and just like he had planned the media trucks and cameras were right on time to get coverage of the raid. "Detective Fuller . . . how did you do this so smoothly when no other law enforcement units could take down the notorious Stephon "Scar" Johnson?" a female reporter screamed out as Derek rushed passed her with Scar in tow.

"It was all in a days' work," Derek wolfed out as he pushed Scar's head down into the back of the police car. Derek looked and felt like a hero. He had taken down the big bad drug kingpin. Derek could not contain himself from smiling. He was the man.

Derek and his unit pulled into the prisoner drop area in the back of the Division 1 stationhouse and unloaded Scar and some of his crew.

"Ay man, when all the pomp and circumstance is done maybe we can break bread, you know, have a drink and shit," Scar said, smiling at Derek mischievously.

"Nah, buddy. You will be breaking bread with your fellow inmates soon enough," Derek said smoothly, slapping five with some of his unit members and walking away leaving Scar to be processed.

Derek continued to slap fives and crack jokes with his unit as they proceeded into the stationhouse. Pushing open the door they heard whistles and applause . . . "Hooray! Hip, hip Hooray!" It was like the other officers and staff at the stationhouse had planned a surprise party. They had all stopped to turn and see the great D.E.S. unit. They were all cheering and whistling loudly. Derek could not contain his proud smile. He loved the attention, especially when he noticed Chief William Scott standing in front of the uproarious crowd. The chief stepped forward, placing his hands up to quiet the cheers so he could speak. He loved to hear himself speak.

"Here they are . . . the untouchable D.E.S. They have done in one day what no other law enforcement agency in Maryland State and the Feds have tried to do for years! Led by one of the finest Detectives in state trooper history . . . Derek Fuller," Chief Scott announced, placing one hand on Derek's shoulder and grabbing his other hand for a firm handshake. The station house crowd of state troopers and administrative staff erupted in cheers again. Derek bowed his head slightly, trying to act modest. Inside, he loved the attention. He basked in it. It was what he had waited so long for . . . to be considered great. He returned the chief's handshake. "I couldn't have done it without the best unit around—Rodriguez, Bolden, Archie and Cassell . . . thank you all for being brave soldiers. This take down was the hard work of us all . . . we have all dedicated countless man hours in the pursuit of justice and now today is our day," Derek said for good measure. In his head he was thinking, it was all him, he had really single handedly taken Scar down, but he knew he had to show good face in front of the chief. This was his case.

"Come down to my office Detective Fuller . . . I want

to speak to you," Chief Scott leaned into Derek's ear and whispered as the crowd began to break up and surround the other unit members. Derek's heart jumped in his chest. Everyone knew that Maryland State Troopers had a history of being prejudiced against any other race other than whites. The fact that this white chief—who was known to be a red neck, wanted to speak to Derek alone, made Derek feel important. It was all working out exactly as Derek had envisioned it.

He followed the chief downstairs to his office. Once inside the chief offered Derek a seat on his famed leather couch—another rare occurrence. Usually an invitation to Chief Scott's office was only for troopers to get an ass chewing or disciplinary action taken against them.

Chief Scott slid his fat stomach behind his desk, put a finger full of chewing tobacco into his cheek and looked at Derek seriously. "Detective Fuller. I don't call many people to my office for compliments. But what you did today was beyond remarkable. Taking down one of the biggest bastard drug lords the state of Maryland has ever seen was more than a simple task. Those fucking DEA federal bastards couldn't do it this long with all their corrupt agents and pay offs. You have exceeded any expectations I had ever dreamed for D.E.S. and for that I commend you. Detective Fuller, I truly think you have what it takes to be higher up in the department one day . . . maybe even sit at this desk as chief, " Chief Scott said seriously, spitting his gooey chewed up tobacco into a can on his desk. Derek was glowing from the accolades he was receiving.

"Well chief, I appreciate the compliment. I just want to work hard and continue to make you and the department proud. It took months of surveillance and lots of footwork on the streets . . . but at the end of the day, that bastard Scar Johnson deserved to go down. I'm just glad it is over," Derek replied, standing up. "Now, after I finish the paperwork I'm going home to my beautiful family who I have neglected for the last six months. I'm sure my wife will be happy to see me," Derek said, smiling just thinking about his beautiful wife.

"I've seen your wife. I would be on my way home too," Chief Scott commented, with a smile sending Derek on his way.

Derek turned his key in the door to his modest single-family home and he could already smell the sweet smells of his dinner wafting through the house. He loved his wife so much. She was a triple threat—a good mother, a working professional and a damned good wife. "Hello?!" Derek called out and then waited.

"Daddy! Daddy!" he heard his kids screaming as they ran towards him top speed. They were not used to him being home at night. Most of the time he would come in after a long stakeout and they would already be asleep, so his presence was a welcomed surprise.

"Ayyy baby girl and my big man," Derek sang, picking up his two-year old daughter and rubbing his six year old son's head.

"We saw you on the news today!" his son announced

proudly, holding onto his father like he never wanted him to leave again. With kids hanging onto him, Derek moved slowly toward the kitchen where he knew Tiphani waited for him. Just like he expected, his sexy wife stood by the stove with her back turned, her long jet-black hair lying on her back and her apple-bottom looking perfect in her fitted jeans. Derek put his daughter down and grabbed his wife around her waist from the back. He inhaled her strawberry shampoo and tucked her hair behind her ear so he could kiss the smooth skin of her neck. She smiled.

"Hey, hey . . . you have to wait for all of that," she sang, putting her stirring spoon down and turning to greet her hero-husband properly.

"Well hurry up and feed these rug rats so I won't have to wait too long," Derek whispered in her ear. He could feel his nature rising. After almost ten years of marriage he was still attracted to his wife like they had just begun dating. He never grew tired or bored with her and it was a plus that she kept herself looking right with regular manicures, pedicures, and facials. In his line of work, divorce was rampant but Derek and Tiphani had stood the test of time. Derek was grateful to have a partner who understood that sometimes his work had to come first and he gave her the same respect.

After dinner Derek tucked the kids into bed while Tiphani cleaned up the dishes. As soon as the little ones drifted off, Derek snuck back downstairs and watched his wife's sexy frame move around the kitchen. Shaking his head left to right, Derek was in awe of her beautiful, flawless caramel skin, her chinky almond shaped eyes, and beautiful hourglass figure. He rushed into the kitchen and grabbed her roughly, lifting her off her feet. "Wait silly . . . let's go upstairs," she giggled.

"I can't wait anymore. Seeing your ass in them jeans got me on rock!" Derek exclaimed, fumbling with the button on her jeans. She acquiesced, throwing her hands around his neck. Derek hoisted her onto their granite countertop and yanked her jeans off, pulling her black lace thong off with them. He inhaled, excited by the sight of her beautifully trimmed triangle. "Fuck . . . you look so damn good! I missed you baby!" he huffed, barely able to contain himself. Tiphani licked her fingers seductively and rubbed her clitoris, causing it to swell slightly. Derek had finally got his own pants off. His medium-sized member stood at full attention. He was a firm believer it wasn't the size that mattered . . . it was what you did with what you had that made all the difference. Derek rushed over to her and began licking the inside of her thighs.

"Ahh," Tiphani grunted, throwing her head back. Derek teased around her thighs until she took her hand and forced his head between her legs. He stuck his tongue out and licked her clit softly. Tiphani slid her hot box towards his tongue in ecstasy. "I want you," she whispered. At that, Derek lifted his head, grabbed his dick and drove it into his wife's soaking wet opening with full force. She let out a short gasp as Derek dug further into her flesh. Tiphani dug her nails into his shoulders. He began to pump harder. Suddenly something happened. Derek recoiled slightly. Tiphani closed her legs around his back trying to keep him inside her. She was hoping that it didn't happen again.

"Urgghhh!!!" Derek growled, collapsing. Tiphani slouched her shoulders and lowered her head. He had cum less than two minutes after it had all started. "Fuck!" he cursed himself, his cheeks flaming over with embarrassment.

"I'm so sorry baby, I was just so excited to feel you," Derek said, making excuses for his shortcomings.

"I know you were just excited. That shit was still good baby," Tiphani consoled as she hugged him.

"Did you at least cum?" Derek asked.

Is he fuckin' kidding me with that question? Tiphani screamed silently in her head. "Hell yeah, baby . . . you know I cum as soon as you touch me," she lied, as she hugged him and hid her face. Derek continued to apologize and she continued to console him. *This shit is so out of control right now!* Tiphani thought to herself as she rolled her eyes behind Derek's back. It wasn't like he came fast and stayed hard where he could please her too. After his nut he was a goner, leaving her unsatisfied and royally pissed the fuck off. Derek didn't know if she was telling the truth, but he did know that his premature ejaculation was starting to become a problem.

Chapter 2

Tables Turned

It had been three months since the raid and the day had finally come. Security was tight as Derek walked up to the courthouse. He could hardly make it to the steps there were so many reporters and spectators outside. Scar's impending trial had been in the news for weeks. There had even been a countdown of sorts. The media had dubbed it the "Trial of the Year." When some of the media hounds noticed Derek they almost trampled each other to be the first to get a statement from him.

"Detective Fuller are you nervous to face the notorious Stephon "Scar" Johnson?" a reporter called out shoving a microphone into Derek's face.

"Are you kidding me with that question? If I wasn't nervous to bring him down in his own hood, why would I be nervous about facing him in a court of law?" Derek replied, giving the reporter a bit of heat. After he set the media straight, Derek smoothed the front of his Brooks Brothers suit and continued his stride up the courthouse steps.

It was no better inside the courtroom than outside.

There were throngs of cameras and reporters lined up around the back and sides. Derek sat on the bench directly behind the prosecutor's table and looked around. He could feel more than one pair of icy eyes on him. There were numerous members of Scar's crew peppered throughout the courtroom crowd and they weren't hiding their glares. Derek turned around just in time to see the court officers leading Scar to the defendant's table. Scar had a huge smile plastered on his face and he stared directly at Derek. Derek surveyed Scar and shook his head. "Ain't this a bitch?" Derek mumbled when he noticed that Scar donned an expensive Armani suit, complete with a tailor-made French cuff shirt, diamond cuff links and to top it off, what looked to be an authentic Cuban cigar sticking out of the breast pocket of his suit jacket. Scar looked down at his suit and back over at Derek. Speaking with his eyes and facial expression, Scar was letting Derek know he was still the man regardless of the bust.

"All rise . . . the honorable Judge Irvin Klein presiding in the matter of the state of Maryland versus Stephon Johnson," the court officer called out. Everyone in the courtroom began to stand up. Derek broke his gaze on Scar, turned around and stood up as the judge slid into his seat on the bench. With a bang of his gavel the judge started the highly anticipated court proceedings. An eerie hush fell over the courtroom and all eyes were front and center.

"Is the state ready to present its case? If so, prosecutor Fuller you may begin . . ." Judge Klein began. On cue, the prosecutor, who Derek thought was the most beautiful, sexy, caramel specimen of a woman he had ever laid eyes on stood up to start. *My wife is not only beautiful she is on point. She got this shit.* Derek thought to himself, smiling proudly. She moved her sexy frame from behind the table and opened her mouth, but before she could speak Scar's defense lawyer—a shark named Larry Tillman jumped to his feet.

"Your honor, I would like to move to have this case dismissed immediately!" Mr. Tillman screamed out. Everyone in the courtroom was looking at him like he was crazy. Not only was he interrupting the prosecutor, he was stepping on the toes of one of the most hard ass judges in the Maryland court system. Hushed murmurs passed amongst the onlookers.

"Mr. Tillman . . . you will speak when spoken to," Judge Klein said.

"Your honor with all due respect, I am requesting to approach the bench," Mr. Tillman said. Prosecutor Fuller looked around confused. She was seething mad. She ran her hands over her skirt and cocked her head to the side in an attempt to compose herself.

"Your honor please tell me you will not allow the defense to turn this trial into a side show," she said through clenched teeth.

"Approach!" the judge screamed.

Derek looked around confused. Scar was smiling from ear to ear. The media was going crazy writing and recording. The two attorneys approached the bench. The judge leaned in and spoke to them while everyone else seemed to be holding their breath waiting to see what would happen next.

Then the judge spoke somberly. "Mr. Tillman you may proceed with your argument for dismissal," the judge said.

"I would be glad to," Tillman replied, smiling like a Cheshire cat.

"Your honor with all due respect. I am asking that the state's case against my client Stephon Johnson be dismissed and that the evidence obtained be deemed inadmissible as it was obtained without warrant, and without consent to search. Therefore was obtained through an illegal search and seizure, which you and I both know was a direct and despicable violation of my client's fourth amendment rights. The state and their rogue cowboy troopers showed no writ of probable cause to enter my client's property and seize property or persons contained therein. This case was a prime example of the Maryland state troopers constant attempt at racial profiling and prejudice against young men like my client. I move to have this case dismissed without prejudice and expunged from my client's record," Mr. Tillman argued. Tiphani Fuller looked back at her husband, her face contorted with confusion and anger. *He told me it was all good, he better be right,* she thought.

Loud gasps and murmurs erupted in the courtroom as Scar's attorney laid out his argument. Derek gripped the bottom of the wooden bench he sat on so hard his knuckles turned white. Chief Scott and the entire D.E.S unit sat in the back of the courtroom and were up in arms as they heard the defense basically make them look like racist assholes. Scar just sat there with a smug look on his face. Knowing he was about to be set free.

"Order! Order!" Judge Klein screamed out banging his gavel over and over. Finally, things quieted down in the courtroom. "In light of this new and unsettling revelation and the fact that the court records did not reflect that a search and seizure warrant was returned to this court, I have no choice but to honor the U.S. Constitution, in accordance with the fourth amendment—which provides citizens the right to be free from illegal search and seizure. I hearby dismiss the state's case against defendant, Stephon Johnson on the grounds that the state's evidence is inadmissible in the nature it was obtained," Judge Klein said regretfully, slamming his gavel and rushing up from the bench.

The courtroom erupted into pandemonium. Reporters scrambled to get the best shot of Derek and Scar. Tiphani threw her papers on the desk and stood up enraged. The D.E.S members and Scar's henchmen began exchanging harsh words and the court officers were overwhelmed with trying to bring order in the courthouse. Derek hung his head in shame. His wife shot him evil looks. She had put her ass on the line for this case. Chief Scott rushed over to him and grabbed him up by the arm. "I need to talk to you Detective Fuller . . . now!" Chief Scott growled, pulling Derek into the hallway by his arm. "For Christ sake Fuller what the fuck were you thinking?! Something as simple as getting a fucking warrant!" Chief Scott said in a harsh whisper.

"I thought that Cassell had gotten the warrant. I read

the fuckin' probable cause affidavit . . . I just knew he had it!" Derek lied. The truth was he never bothered to check. He was so gung ho that he did not follow up like he should have and now the whole entire case was a waste. "Chief . . . I can fix this . . ." Derek started.

"You let the department down. You better come up with some good shit to redeem yourself Fuller," Chief Scott said. Just then a huge, uproarious crowd began moving towards them. It was like the scene around a hot celebrity surrounded by fans. Derek and the chief looked on and in the middle of the crowd stood Scar. He could not contain the still smug smile that spread on his face as he held his unlit Cuban cigar between his fingers. As the crowd, complete with media cameras and Scar's henchmen approached Derek, Scar stopped.

"If it ain't the fuckin' man without a plan," Scar said sarcastically to Derek winking. That was it.

"Fuck you!" Derek screamed, lunging at Scar. Derek instinctively reached into his waistline for his weapon. When he felt nothing there he realized that when he entered the courthouse he had to check in his gun.

"You lucky bastard!" Derek grumbled as Chief Scott blocked him. Scar's crew had gotten ready for battle, stepping in front of Scar ready to take on Derek. Chief Scott continued to struggle to restrain Fuller.

"Fuller! This bastard is not fucking worth it," the chief said, dragging a raging Derek down the opposite end of the courthouse hallway. Scar popped his collar and stepped across the courthouse threshold into freedom.

A GIRL FROM FLINT

Prologue

Karma is what put me in that hellhole. I don't even know how I ended up in jail. A couple years ago I was on top of the world. I've had more money flow through my hands than most people ever see in their entire lives. I was the woman that everybody wanted, and I had my way with some of the richest men in the Midwest. From prestigious businessmen to the most hood-rich niggas in Flint, I've had them all.

We thought it was a game, and in a way it was. We were trained to be the best. Skilled in the art of seduction, we were professionals who knew how to please in every sexual way. In my family the mentality was if you ain't fucking, you don't eat.Growing up in the hood, I had to use what I had to get what I wanted. My pussy was my meal ticket, and in order to stay on top, I juiced every nigga green to the game. I felt like, if a dude was stupid enough to let me trick him out of his dough, then he deserved to get got. "Fuck me, pay me" was our motto, and I used to laugh when my girls used to shout that after we hustled men out of their money.

It's not quite as funny these days though. Now I've got a prison sentence hanging over my head, and I'm locked in this cage like an animal. I haven't washed my hair in months, and I'm looking over my shoulder every minute of every day, hoping these bitches in here won't try to get at me. I don't know, maybe it was my destiny. All the wrong that I've done, all that shit came back like a boomerang and hit me harder than I could have ever imagined. I sit in this jail cell every day wondering how I landed in a state prison, a maximum-security state prison at that.

When I heard the judge say those words, it brought tears to my eyes. It was like a nightmare and I was dreaming about my worst fear—only I couldn't wake up. It was real, and there was no waking up from it.

My downfall was . . . well, you'll learn about that later.

From the very beginning of my life, I was headed in a downward spiral. My mother is a crack fiend, and I haven't seen or spoken to her in years. I never knew my father. He died before I got the chance to get to know him. I hear that he really loved me, but the fact that he wasn't in my life affected me. I never had that male figure in my life, and that pains me greatly.

As you read this novel, understand that this is what happened to me, and that everything that you do has its consequences.

I remember we would talk about opening up our own salon and not needing a nigga to support us. That was before my life got complicated. Believe me, if I could turn back the hands of time, I would have never stepped foot in the murder capital—Flint, Michigan. Yeah, that was the first of our mistakes. Honey made it seem so live, so wonderful. I thought it was the city that would make all my dreams come true. The truth of the matter is, everyone in that damn city has hidden agendas and is looking for a way to get paid, by any means necessary. I was a little girl trying to do big things in a small city. I should've just kept my ass in good ol' New York.

Me and my girls thought we were the shit. We got whatever we wanted, when we wanted it, from dick to pocketbooks, even first-class vacations around the world. We used men until their pockets ran out, and when we were done, we tossed them aside and moved along to the next. Some people may call us hoes, gold-diggers, or even high-paid prostitutes, but nah, it wasn't like that. It was our hustle, and trust me, it paid well. Very well.

I wish I could go back to the good ol' days when we used to smoke weed in Amra's room and open the windows so Ms. Pat wouldn't find out. Or the days when we used to lie about staying the night over each other's houses so we could go to parties and stay out all night. Those are the memories that make this place bearable.

Those are the times that I reflect on when I get depressed and when life seems unfair. The times when it was just me, Honey, Amra, and Mimi, the original Manolo Mamis. There have been many after us, but none like us. All them other bitches are just watered-down versions of what we used to be. That's who we were, that was our clique. That's the friendship that I miss, and think about when I feel lonely. The thought of how close we used to be is something I will cherish forever.

I know I'm rambling on and on about me and my girlfriends. You are probably wondering, *Bitch, how did you end up in jail?* Damn, I'm so busy trying to tell y'all what happened, I forgot to introduce myself. I know y'all wanna read about Halleigh and Malek and all that high-school bullshit, but let me get my piece off first. I promise you, you won't be disappointed. I'm Tasha, and this is my Flint story.

Chapter One

1994

As Lisa looked into the mirror, she could not recognize the eyes that stared back at her. Everything started running through her mind all at once. She thought about the loss of her only love, Ray, his death, and about their creation, Tasha. Tasha was the only positive thing in her life. Her bloodshot eyes stared into the mirror as she looked into her lifeless soul and began to cry.

Lisa tied a brown leather belt around her arm and began to slap her inner arm with two fingers, desperately searching for a vein. As the tears of guilt streamed down her face, she looked at the heroin-filled needle on the sink and reached for it. She hated that she had this terrible habit, but it called for her. She wasn't shooting up to get high anymore; she was doing it to feel better. She needed the drug. She tried to resist it, but the drug called out to her more and more. When she wasn't high, she was sick and in tremendous pain, and her body fiended for it.

She injected the dope into her vein and a warm sensation traveled up her arm. The tears seemed to stop instantly, and her frail body slowly slumped to the floor, her eyes staring up into space. All of Lisa's emotions and her negative thoughts slowly escaped her mind as she began to smirk. She could not shake this habit that a former boyfriend had introduced her to, and her weekend binges eventually became an addiction.Her addiction affected her life, as well as her daughter's. All of her welfare checks sponsored the local dope man's chrome rims, ice, and pocket money.

Her life started going downhill after the death of Raymond Parks, better known as Ray. It was 1982, the era of pimping. Lisa was fifteen when she met Ray, who was twenty-one at the time and a known pimp in the area. Ray approached Lisa while she was walking to the store. He pulled up and slyly said, "Hey, sweetness. Wanna ride?"

Lisa paid him no mind and kept walking. She started switching her ass a little harder while walking, knowing she had an audience. She pretended not to be flattered by the older man and flipped her sandy-brown hair.

Ray parked his long Cadillac at the corner and stepped his shiny gators onto the streets of Queens. He took his time and eventually caught up with the thick young woman with hazel eyes. He slid in front of Lisa, blocking her path.

"Hello, beautiful. My name is Raymond, but my friends call me Ray. I wouldn't have forgiven myself if I didn't take the time out to meet you." Ray stuck out his hand and offered a handshake.

Lisa looked up and saw a tall, lean, brown-skinned

young man. She couldn't stop her lips from spreading, and she unleashed her pretty smile. She shook his hand and said with a shaky voice, "I'm Lisa."

Raymond smiled and stared into her eyes. Lisa stared back, and her eyes couldn't seem to leave his. He knew he had her when he saw that all too familiar look in her eyes. He asked in a smooth, calm voice, "Can I take you out sometime?"

"My mama might not like that."

Ray smiled. "Just let me handle her. So, can I take you out sometime or what?"

Lisa blushed. "Yeah, I guess that'll be all right."

Raymond gave her his number and asked her how old she was. Lisa told him that she was only fifteen. Ray's facial expression dropped, disappointed to know she was so young. He didn't usually approach girls her age, but she had an adult body and was by far the most beautiful girl he'd ever seen. He grabbed her hand, looked at her, and told her to give him a call so he could pick her up later that day.

Lisa watched Ray get into his car and pull off. She couldn't stop smiling to herself as she continued to walk to the store. *He was a fly brother. I hope my momma let me go.* She hurried to the store so she could get home and call Ray. She knew that it would take a miracle for her to get her mother's approval, but as fine as Ray was, she was definitely going to try.

***

Lisa called Ray later that evening, and an hour later he was at her front door with a dozen roses in each hand. Lisa's mother answered the door and was impressed by the well-dressed young man that stood before her. She noticed he wasn't around Lisa's age and became skeptical about letting him in.

Ray sensed the vibe and quickly worked his magic. He handed the flowers to her and took off his hat to show respect.

Ray didn't get to take Lisa out that night. He and Lisa's mother talked, and he charmed her for hours. He barely spoke to Lisa the entire evening. A professional at sweet-talking, he knew that to get Lisa, he had to get her mother first.

As the night came to an end, Ray said good-bye to Lisa's mother and asked if Lisa could walk him to his car. She agreed, and they exited the house.

Lisa and Ray stood in the driveway. He took her by the hand and said, "I never saw a lady so fly. I want you to be mine . . . eventually. What school do you go to?"

"McKinley."

Ray shook his head then said in a soft voice, "I know where that's at. I'll pick you up after school tomorrow, okay?"

Lisa started to cheese. "Really?"

He grabbed Lisa's head, kissed her forehead softly, and whispered, "See you tomorrow."

She turned around and entered her mother's house, and Ray took off as soon as he saw that she got in safely.

***

The next day Ray was parked outside of the high school in his Cadillac, waiting for his new "pretty young thang," as he called her.

When she got into the car, Ray smiled at her. "Hello, beautiful. How was your day?"

From that day on, Ray and Lisa were together. He took her on shopping sprees weekly, and she was happy with her man. He never asked for sex and never rushed or pressured her in any way. Lisa wondered why the subject never came up and wondered if he was physically attracted to her. Ray was very much attracted to her, but he'd promised himself he wouldn't touch her until she was eighteen. He had his hoes and women all over town, so sex was never an issue.

Lisa knew about his other women and his line of work, but never complained. Ray took care of her and treated her like a queen at all times. Over time, she fell deeply in love with him, and never had a desire to mess with any other man.

Ray always made sure she had whatever she wanted and that she went to school every day. If she didn't do well in school, her gifts would stop, so Lisa became a very good student.

Occasionally Ray would help Lisa's mother with bills and put food in their refrigerator. Ray had money, real money. He was a pimp with hoes all over the city. He wasn't the type to put his hands on a woman. He made exceptions for the hoes that played with his chips or disrespected him, but in general, he had mind control over many women, so violence was rarely needed.

Exactly one month after her eighteenth birthday, Lisa found out she was pregnant with Ray's child. She couldn't believe she had gotten knocked up on her first time, but when she told Ray, he was the happiest man on earth. Lisa dropped out of school, and Ray immediately moved her from her mother's house and into his plush home in the suburbs.

He used to put his head on Lisa's stomach every night and tended to her every need. He promised that when he saved up enough money, he would open a business and exit the pimping game.

Eight months into her pregnancy, Lisa began to become jealous of Ray and all his women, and confronted him about it.Ray reacted in a way that Lisa never saw. He raised his voice and said, "Don't worry about me and my business! You just have my baby girl and stand by yo' man!" He stormed out of the house and slammed the front door.

Lisa felt bad for confronting him and began to cry. She cried for hours because she'd upset the only man she ever loved. Ray was all she knew. She stayed up and waited for his return, but he never came.

That night Ray went around town to collect his money from his workers. He was upset with himself for raising his voice at Lisa. He'd never yelled at her before, so it was really bothering him.

He pulled his Cadillac onto York Avenue and saw one of his best workers talking with a heavyset man about to turn a trick. He thought to himself, *Make that cheddar, Candy.* He decided to wait until Candy finished her business before collecting from her. He sat back in his seat and turned the ignition off, sat back and listened to the smooth sounds of the Isley Brothers and slowly rocked his head.

He looked back at Candy and noticed that the man and Candy were entering a car parked on the opposite side of the street. Candy was his "bottom bitch." She always kept cash flowing and never took days off. He smiled. *Candy going to make that fool cum in thirty seconds.*

Suddenly he saw Candy jump out of the car, spitting and screaming at the man. She walked toward the sidewalk spitting. The man jumped out of the car and started to yell at Candy, and yelled even louder when Candy kept on walking.

At this point, Ray calmly stepped out of the car and began to head toward her. The man had gotten to Candy and grabbed her and was screaming at the top of his lungs. Ray approached the man from behind and grabbed him. "Relax, relax."

"Mind yo' fucking business, playa. This bitch is trying to juke me out of my money."

"Daddy Ray, he pissed in my mouth! He didn't say shit about pissing. I don't get down like that."

Before Ray could say anything, the man lunged at Candy, slamming her head hard into the brick wall she was leaning on. Ray immediately grabbed the man by the neck and began to choke him. His fingers wrapped tightly around his neck, Ray whispered to him, "Never put your hands on my hoes. If I see you around here again, it's you and me, youngblood." Ray released the man, and he dropped to the ground, trying to catch his breath. Ray stood over the man and pulled out a money clip full of cash. "How much did you give her?"

"Forty. I gave her forty," the man said, rubbing his neck.

Ray peeled off two twenties and threw it at the man and told him to get the fuck out of his office. The man took the money and ran to his car and pulled off.

Ray then turned around to help Candy up. She was lying motionless. He quickly bent down to aid her and noticed she wasn't breathing. He started to shake her and call her name. "Candy! Candy!" He got no response.

He gave her mouth to mouth resuscitation, and she began to breathe lightly. He knew he had to get her to the hospital, but he didn't want to be the one to take her in. It would raise suspicion if a known pimp brought a half-dressed hooker in, barely breathing and battered. He decided to go in her purse to see if he could find a number for someone that she knew, to check her into the hospital.

As soon as he stuck his hand in her purse, he saw flashing lights and heard a man on a bullhorn telling him to put his hands up. Then another police car pulled up.

Ray stood up, both of his hands in the air.

One of the police officers ran to the girl and put his fingers on her neck. He shook his head. The policemen handcuffed Ray and began to read him his rights.

"Wait, man, you got this all wrong—"

"Yeah, yeah." The cop led Ray to this police car.

Ray began to pull away from him. "Listen, I was helping her. I didn't—"

Another cop hit Ray over the head with a billy club. "You got caught red-handed robbing this young lady. People like you make me sick."

Ray was too dazed to say anything as the cops put him in the back of the police car. He knew it looked bad for him. He dropped his head and began to pray.

The prosecutor stood up to give his closing argument. He wiped his forehead with a handkerchief then slowly approached the jury. "The man sitting in that defendant chair is a man of no remorse. He killed a seventeen-year-old girl in cold blood. Imagine if that girl was your daughter, your sister, or a beloved neighborhood child." He paused for effect. He wanted to give the jury time to process what he'd just said.

He pointed his finger at Ray. "This man is a menace to society and deserves to be punished to the fullest extent of the law. All of the evidence points toward one man, and that man is sitting before us today. That man is Raymond Parks.

"Nothing can keep our communities safe from this

tyrant except a life sentence. The only people who can make that happen are you, the people of the jury. Don't put another young girl in danger. Put him away for the rest of his life. He was caught over his victim's dead body, rummaging through her purse, looking for money. He drove this woman's skull against a brick wall so hard and so violently, her brain hemorrhaged, which ultimately led to her death. How cold-blooded is that? So the prosecution asks of you—no, we beg of you—the jury to sentence this man to a lifetime in prison. Render a guilty verdict and bring justice back to the community. I rest my case."

The prosecuting attorney turned and walked back to his seat, a smug grin on his face. He knew he'd just delivered a closing argument that would cripple the defense and win the trial.

Ray looked back at Lisa and her swollen belly and felt an agonizing pain in his heart. He might spend the rest of his life in jail for a crime he didn't commit. He felt tears well up in his eyes as he mouthed the words, "I love you," to Lisa.

Lisa looked into Ray's eyes and began to cry. She knew that the chances were slim for him to get off. She gripped the bench she was sitting on. *Please, God, let them find him not guilty. Please . . . I need him,* she prayed as the jury deliberated in a private room.

Half an hour later, the jury returned to the courtroom with the verdict. An overweight old white man stood up and looked into Raymond's eyes and said, "We, the jury, find the defendant, Raymond J. Parks, guilty of murder in the second degree and guilty of strong-armed robbery."

Lisa screamed when the verdict was pronounced.

Ray dropped his head as the guards came over to escort him out of the courtroom. He looked at his attorney. "That's it? You said you could beat this case. I'm innocent, man. I'm innocent."

His attorney looked at him, shrugged his shoulders, and gave a sly smile. "We'll file an appeal."

Ray knew that his chances of winning the appeal would be just as slim as his chances of winning the trial. He looked at Lisa as they carried him out of the courtroom. "I love you," he mouthed again as the guards handcuffed him.

Lisa felt so much pain in her heart. She just stood there and watched her only love leave her life. Helpless, she didn't know what to do. Ray was going to prison, and there was nothing she could do to stop it from happening.

She was so distraught, she couldn't control herself. She felt her dress become soaked and thought she had peed on herself. She felt liquid run down her leg and then realized it wasn't urine. Her water had broken. "I'm going into labor," she screamed to Ray just as the guards took him from her sight.

Her mother told her to sit down and then called a guard over for help.

Later that evening, Tasha Parks was born. It was the worst day of Lisa's life. The love of her life had been convicted of murder, and ironically, their child was born on the same day.

Lisa was depressed for months and cried herself to sleep every night with her newborn baby in her arms. Ray left behind a house and some money in the bank, so she supported herself and her daughter with that.

Lisa visited Ray as soon as they let her. He had grown a beard and walked to the table where a thick glass window separated them. She picked up the phone, and so did Ray. Ray did not have the same look in his eye that he used to have. The sparkle had diminished. Lisa desperately looked, trying to find a piece of the man she had fallen in love with, but it wasn't there. He had changed. There was no warm feeling in his eyes anymore, only coldness.

"How are you?" she asked, trying to be supportive.

Ray shook his head and smiled. "Don't worry about me. Just make sure you take care of our child. Lisa, I'm gon' be in here for a long time. I love you, and I want you to always remember that. I'll love you to the day I die."

Lisa noticed his hopeless vibe. It seemed as if he were telling her good-bye forever. "You're coming home, baby. Your lawyer is gon' file an appeal, and you're coming home."

Ray had to stop himself from becoming emotional. "That appeal is bullshit, baby. They are going to find me guilty, just like they did this time. That's even if the judge grants an appeal. Just remember, I love you, and don't let my baby girl grow up not knowing that I love her too."

Lisa looked at their daughter and then at Ray. "Tasha and I need you, Ray. You're all we got. We need you." She put her hand on the glass.

A single tear streamed down Ray's face. "*Tasha*? That's my baby girl's name? Make sure you tell her I love her. Every day, make sure that she knows that." He arose from his seat, kissed his fingers, and pressed them against the glass. He then began to walk out.

Lisa gripped the phone tightly and banged it against the glass, "No!" she screamed. "Ray, I love you! I love you!"

Ray walked back over to the glass and picked up the phone. "I love you, Lisa, but don't come here again. I don't want you or my daughter to see me in here. You deserve more. I love you." With those words, he headed to the cage that would be his home for the rest of his life.

A few weeks later, Lisa was breast-feeding Tasha when she received a phone call. She felt the floor spinning as she tried to understand the news from the other end. When she was sure she'd heard what the voice said, she dropped the phone and fell to her knees, her baby in the other arm. "No!" she screamed as she cried. Tasha was startled by her mother's roar and began to cry too.

Ray had been stabbed fifteen times in the chest by an fellow inmate.

***

Lisa sank into a deep depression and moved back home with her mother after Ray's death. She would go for weeks at a time without talking to anyone or even bathing. She often blamed herself for Ray's death, believing he wouldn't have stormed out of the house if she hadn't confronted him that night. *He would have stayed home with me,* she often thought to herself.

Lisa, looking for the same love that Ray had shown her, began to let men manipulate her into doing what they pleased. Any man who dressed nice and approached her had a chance. It became a problem when her mother grew tired of caring for Tasha while Lisa ran the streets.

Four years after Ray's death, another death was about to hit Lisa: her mother's.

When Lisa's mother died, she finally felt the burden of being a mother. Tasha had grown so attached to her grandmother, she even thought she was her mother, calling her Mama, and Lisa by her first name.

Lisa met a man by the name of Glenn, a pimp in the neighborhood. He was in no way as successful as Ray, but Lisa was drawn to him. In some way, he reminded her of Ray.

Glenn introduced Lisa to weed. She liked the way it made her feel and began to smoke it so much, it didn't get her high anymore.

Then he introduced her to cocaine, telling her, "It

makes you feel good." Lisa used to snort a little cocaine with Glenn, but that quickly grew old. Eventually she needed a new high, and Glenn provided that too. And so it was that she got hooked on heroin.

ORDER FORM
URBAN BOOKS, LLC
78 E. Industry Ct
Deer Park, NY 11729

Name: (please print): _____

Address: _____

City/State: _____

Zip: _____

QTY	TITLES	PRICE
	The Cartel	$14.95
	The Cartel#2	$14.95
	The Dopeman's Wife	$14.95
	The Prada Plan	$14.95
	Gunz And Roses	$14.95
	Snow White	$14.95
	A Pimp's Life	$14.95
	Hush	$14.95
	Little Black Girl Lost 1	$14.95
	Little Black Girl Lost 2	$14.95
	Little Black Girl Lost 3	$14.95
	Little Black Girl Lost 4	$14.95

Shipping and Handling - add $3.50 for 1st book then $1.75 for each additional book.

Please send a check payable to:

Urban Books, LLC

Please allow 4 - 6 weeks for delivery

ORDER FORM
URBAN BOOKS, LLC
78 E. Industry Ct
Deer Park, NY 11729

Name: (please print):_____

Address: _____

City/State: _____

Zip: _____

QTY	TITLES	PRICE
	A Man's Worth	$14.95
	Abundant Rain	$14.95
	Battle Of Jericho	$14.95
	By The Grace Of God	$14.95
	Dance Into Destiny	$14.95
	Divorcing The Devil	$14.95
	Forsaken	$14.95
	Grace And Mercy	$14.95
	Guilty & Not Guilty Of Love	$14.95
	His Woman, His Wife His Widow	$14.95
	Illusion	$14.95
	The LoveChild	$14.95

Shipping and Handling - add $3.50 for 1st book then $1.75 for each additional book.

Please send a check payable to:

Urban Books, LLC

Please allow 4 - 6 weeks for delivery

ORDER FORM
URBAN BOOKS, LLC
78 E. Industry Ct
Deer Park, NY 11729

Name: (please print): _____

Address: _____

City/State: _____

Zip: _____

QTY	TITLES	PRICE
	16 ½ On The Block	$14.95
	16 On The Block	$14.95
	Betrayal	$14.95
	Both Sides Of The Fence	$14.95
	Cheesecake And Teardrops	$14.95
	Denim Diaries	$14.95
	Happily Ever Now	$14.95
	Hell Has No Fury	$14.95
	If It Isn't love	$14.95
	Last Breath	$14.95
	Loving Dasia	$14.95
	Say It Ain't So	$14.95

Shipping and Handling - add $3.50 for 1st book then $1.75 for each additional book.

Please send a check payable to:

Urban Books, LLC

Please allow 4 - 6 weeks for delivery

ORDER FORM
URBAN BOOKS, LLC
78 E. Industry Ct
Deer Park, NY 11729

Name:(please print):_____

Address: _____

City/State: _____

Zip: _____

QTY	TITLES	PRICE

Shipping and Handling - add $3.50 for 1st book then $1.75 for each additional book.

Please send a check payable to:

Urban Books, LLC

Please allow 4 - 6 weeks for delivery

Notes

Notes